# Once in Two Lifetimes

**The Current Mr. Orr, Volume 2**

Sean Boling

Published by Sean Boling, 2023.

This is a work of fiction. Similarities to real people, places, or events are entirely coincidental.

ONCE IN TWO LIFETIMES

**First edition. January 3, 2023.**

Copyright © 2023 Sean Boling.

ISBN: 979-8224414475

Written by Sean Boling.

# Chapter One

I know the name of my attorney, but never use it when talking to him. If I do, he gets flustered. We never speak in person, always by phone, usually through a text, but he is easy to read no matter where his voice is coming from. I never give his name to anyone else, either. I just say my attorney is going to be in touch. During my one-afternoon search to poach a lawyer from the company I sold earlier that morning, I was hoping for a candidate who lacked ambition and any interest in social attachments. He had far less of each than I dared wish for. Every round of interviews proved he was everything I wanted, which is why when my phone rings, the screen says there is an incoming call from "Everything".

I answer without any sort of greeting.

Greetings also make him nervous.

"A phone call," I say. "Wow. No text."

"Your former assistant is trying to get in touch with you," he says.

"Kelly?"

"Yes."

"How did she find out you're my lawyer?"

"Could you ask her? She seems very persistent."

"Fine."

"I'll text you the number."

"Speaking of sending me things..."

"Almost done. I'll send you the file tomorrow morning."

"Great."

The call ends.

Nita arrives at the same time with a pitcher of iced tea to refill my half-empty glass.

"Have you ever said good bye to him?" she asks.

"He hangs up before I have a chance."

"What's the latest project?" she raises her voice over the clatter of cascading ice and tea.

Nita is not being nosy. The restaurant closed at two o'clock, they only serve dinner on weekends, and there is nothing left to clean up or clear away other than my empty plate.

"Do you remember the last project?" I ask.

"I most certainly do," she responds with a dry defensiveness. "I don't just make conversations. I commit to them."

"The latest one is an extension of the last one."

"Oh. The charter school."

"They need laptop carts for the classrooms."

She takes my plate with one hand and swipes a towel over the tabletop with her other hand.

"Just the carts?"

"Laptops included," I drown my fake dismay with iced tea.

She grins and disappears with the last dirty dish of her shift. It had been filled with a carnitas burrito and a side of wet fries. I am positive Devin never ordered such a combo during his shift on earth. If he ever did, it was not in a place like this. I indulged in too many earth specials when I first settled into a life lacking public relations or image management, and discovered I was capable of putting on weight as much as the next person. It enhanced my feelings of being human, but at the risk of cutting the experience short.

Today is my cheat day.

I stand at the conclusion of my last sip, walk to the door, and wait for Nita to let me out. Through the window I see the parking lot is full and a slow tournament of vehicles winds their way to wherever their drivers are going, most likely the grocery store, with the smoke shop and clothing outlet not unlikely.

"Till we meet again," I say as Nita finds the right key on a ring crawling with them.

"Tomorrow?" she assumes while spinning the lock.

"Works for me."

We give each other a quick hug before I re-enter the race and she re-locks the door behind me.

When the sidewalk extends beyond the line of businesses in the discount shopping center, I become the only pedestrian walking beside the heavy traffic traveling at highway speeds between stop lights. The occasional driver or passenger gawks at me, as though they thought the sidewalk was more of a guardrail than something to walk on. For some of them it may have more to do with who is doing the walking. I have seen people walk beside this road, or wait for a bus, but they look like they have come from the fields, or are waiting for someone from the fields. The valley surrounding this town grows a tremendous amount of food, but not the kind that lures tourists. Some farm towns market themselves as gardens of paradise, but this one has resigned itself to being more of a berm crawling with dusty rosemary bushes that runs between the curbs of a center divider in the middle of a busy boulevard like the one I am walking along.

I take the first left, which leads to a deserted intersection a block away, all four corners of it hemmed in by concrete walls shielding the housing developments behind them. I cross the barren pavement and walk to the opening in the wall around my neighborhood, a mix of apartments, condominiums, and single-family homes where it is difficult to tell which ones are which.

My phone buzzes with the text from Everything listing Kelly's name and number. I take a detour off the path that leads to my condo and instead head for a picnic table next to the brick charcoal grill nobody uses in the small park teenagers use to get high.

After several rings that have me preparing to leave a message on her voice mail, she answers.

"Hello Kelly," I adjust my plan.

"Devin?" she says. "Doc? I don't know. What should I call you?"

"Probably best we go with Devin."

"I'll try to remember that. Okay. How's philanthropy going?"

"Going well, thank you."

"I bet. Every time I read or hear about a mysterious benefactor I think it's you."

A limited gaggle of teenagers walking home from school takes over the other picnic table on the other side of the grill.

"How did you find my attorney?"

"I still have a friend in HR back at the old company. I asked her if there were any lawyers who left right after you sold."

"Clever."

"Is he okay?"

"Who?"

"Your attorney."

"He's fine. A little uneasy around people."

I watch the teenagers at the next table curse and laugh at each other and I wonder what Everything was like at that age.

"I only talked to him for about thirty seconds," Kelly says. "And it was the most difficult phone conversation of my life."

"He's a wizard with contracts," I defend him as though one of the young knuckleheads from over the grill is the one hurling insults.

"I would hope so."

"What are you doing with yourself these days?" I change the subject.

"Venture capital. Investing in a few startups. A few promising startups."

"Ah."

"Don't worry. This is not one of those calls. I am not looking for partners."

"Good."

"No. I don't make teams. I invest in them."

"What kind of a call is this, then, Kelly?"

She unfurls a long pause, long enough that I focus on the aimless kids without looking at them, which requires staring at random spaces in the distance, which draws me away from remembering why I am on the phone, and with whom.

"This is a difficult kind of call," she reminds me she is there.

"Clearly."

"My Dad is missing."

"Oh."

I face the same direction but stop seeing anything in front of me, and tune out the teens.

"I know you never met him, but Devin did."

"I remember."

"You do?"

Images come together but maintain a maddening amount of space between each other.

"We were in a rental tent," I scan the pieces. "One of those big white ones with plastic windows for outdoor corporate events."

"That's right," she sounds delighted. "The Food Bank fundraiser."

"I don't suppose Devin put that together."

"He threw money at it. He wanted to be seen there."

"I like your Dad," I have a feeling. "Well, Devin liked him. So who knows if I would."

"You would," she insists. "Everyone does."

"I'll be sure to find out when he turns up."

I hear her doing some rhythmic breathing over the top of her phone, generating the energy she thinks she needs.

"Is there something I can do for you?" I get to the point for her.

"There might be," she pushes herself to say.

"Name it."

"I don't think I can explain over the phone. Can we meet?"

"I moved. I'm about two hours away."

"That's fine. I don't mind. I'll come to you. No meeting halfway."

I take a turn of my own holding the phone away from myself to let the hesitation flow. I never meet anyone here. On the rare occasions I visit with beneficiaries in person, I go where they are. Meeting at one of my regular spots would feel like splashing paint on the camouflage I have crafted over the life I lead.

I think of franchises along the freeway and pick one that gives us a fair shot at privacy, a fast food joint where everyone uses the drive-thru, leaving the dining room empty aside from an occasional vagabond sitting next to their backpack on a break from their perpetual hike.

Kelly picks the day.

In the days leading up to it, I call some police officers who have helped me identify strong investments in their jurisdictions. They help me research private investigators who specialize in missing persons, which is what I assume Kelly wants from me.

She is already there when I arrive.

"I left early in case I got lost," she explains as I approach. "I saved us a booth."

The place is as empty as I suspected it would be. Even under duress, she has jokes.

"Always on top of the meeting logistics," I appreciate the spirit I once found annoying. "Even when you're not paid to be."

"Wow," she stands to greet me. "Do clones not age?"

"You're thinking of robots."

We hug with more ease than either of us probably imagined we would, if we imagined hugging at all.

"What do you want?" I ask at the conclusion of our surprise embrace. "I'm buying. You came all this way."

"Give me the number nine with a Dr. Pepper, and since you're picking up the check, curly fries instead of regular."

"You've been clocking the menu."

"I was really early. Only so many phone calls I could take."

I waffle between egg rolls and taquitos, the kinds of items a franchise like this overextends itself on in order to present variety without regard for taste, but they are lower in calories than the burgers, and I am not wasting a cheat day on this menu.

"Egg rolls," I reveal to Kelly when she asks what I ordered upon returning to our private booth.

"Daring choice."

"Makes for good small talk," I fiddle with the edge of the laminated card with our order number on it.

"Okay, I'll bite then. Why, pray tell, order egg rolls in a burger joint?"

"If I'm going to treat myself to a burger, it's not going to be here."

"The clone diet."

"My relationship to food is the most human thing about me."

"I see."

She seems concerned she may have offended me.

"Sorry to hear about your father," I pull focus away from that concern.

"Thank you."

"I don't think I said as much when we spoke over the phone."

"That's okay. It's pretty distracting news."

"How long has it been?"

"About three weeks."

"Any ideas on what might have happened? Where he might be?"

She lapses into the kind of pause that characterized so much of our phone call.

"I think it has to do with his job."

"Really?" I am intrigued to find her with such a strong lead. "What makes you say that?"

"He's in banking. Big-time banking, involved in managing money for dictators."

"Dictators?" my fascination grows. "In the metaphorical sense, or actual leaders of dictatorships?"

"The bank he works for is in bed with the biggest. Name a crook running his country into the ground, and they're probably a client, or one of their pawns is a client. There's a dictator network. They all maintain accounts at the same banks to help each other out. That way they can ignore any sanctions the rest of the world tries to put on them and make the world safe for autocracy."

"And you think your father crossed one of them?"

"He went on a business trip to Croatia, and that's the last anyone heard from him. He was meeting some guys from Turkmenistan, or Tajikistan, one of the former Soviet stans, and hasn't come back since. He was only supposed to be there a couple days."

"Well..." my list of private investigators having been rendered inadequate, I use it to demonstrate my commitment to help. "I've met a lot of interesting people over the past year, and I called on some of them to come up with a list of excellent private detectives."

"Oh," she tries to feign interest.

"I know, this sounds like more of a job for the FBI, or some international agency with impressive initials. I should have asked more questions before doing the research."

"I could have offered more information."

"You're in a tough place."

"I do want your help."

"Great. I'm honored."

"And I do mean your help. From you. Not from any outsider."

"Oh. Okay."

She pauses and I explore the different directions in which she might be taking this, but she cuts her pause short, as if she would prefer I not speculate.

"You went somewhere when you went under," she blurts out.

I stay silent to see how she builds on that bombshell.

"You met Devin. Or maybe you just share his thoughts."

She looks at me for answers. I want to provide them, but at a minimum.

"The more time has passed, the less sure I am of what happened."

Which is true enough, but not enough for Kelly.

"Did you meet him?" she strains. "After he died?"

I take a deep breath, hoping to surface with a sense of whether to reveal or evade.

"Yes," I reveal.

She is none of what I believed someone would be after learning my secret. She is not excited, astonished, nor in awe. She is relieved.

The woman behind the counter calls our number, even though we are the only customers in the room.

I rise to exchange the laminated number for our food and return with a line to soften our bearing.

"These egg rolls actually look pretty good."

I only look at them after saying so, and to my surprise they really do.

Kelly of course could not care less.

"I was hoping you'd be willing to go back and see if my Dad is there."

I take a bite out of curiosity, as I suspect it will be the only one I take, but I taste nothing, overwhelmed with wondering over how she thinks I can get there, wherever she thinks there is.

"I ended up with the extra syringes from the launch when we put you under," she heads into her explanation. "I think Jalen and Gina wanted me to hold the evidence in case something went wrong. I forgot I had them until Dad vanished. Mom went to Maldives to calm down, and my little sister stayed in her dorm at Wellesley because she said the RA was really helping her cope, so the house was empty and I figured we could use the walk-in freezer to keep you fresh while you went under, since all you need to do is see if he's there, you don't have to stay long."

"Hold on…"

"I know, it sounds dangerous…"

"No," I clarify. "Not that, though we'll get to that. I mean the part about international banking, Maldives, Wellesley, houses with walk-in freezers. I had no idea."

"Who else can afford to work as an intern in the valley?"

"Why did we ever move you on to the payroll?"

"Laws."

"I hope you donated your paycheck to charity."

"Net worth aside," she signals a return to the subject, "after calming down and thinking more about the situation, I realized we have to get the cloning company involved. There's no way around it. I'm sure there's more to keeping you in storage than just cold air, and I wouldn't know how to revive you."

"It's also highly unlikely I would have agreed to those conditions."

"Needless to say," she grows exasperated with my glib dance. "I'm trying to let you know how much I've been thinking about this. I didn't suddenly come up with the idea and give you a call. I'm taking it very seriously."

"So where are you now with your planning?"

"I thought maybe I would go in as a representative of Devin, or we would go in together, you playing Devin, and we could tell them the clone has been acting strangely, and we'd like to sideline him for a while, but then figured coming up with stories of the strange behavior would be tricky."

"Perhaps I should rephrase the question."

"I'm getting there," she snaps. "I'm explaining the process of how I simplified my idea."

"It's an elaborate simplification."

She ignores my jab. Her determination grows on me.

"Trying to invent strange stories led me to an epiphany," she proceeds. "The real story is enough. You should be you. We'll keep Devin out of it. Brush that stunt to the side. Don't even bring me. Designate me as your ride to the lab and back. Go in and tell them that with Devin retired and committed to his philanthropy, you have no purpose, and you keep thinking about what happened while you were in hibernation, and you'd like to explore it again. Tell them whatever you're comfortable sharing about your experience, or make something up, and request however much time you need, or however much time you want."

No witty wisecrack comes to mind.

I stop the dance.

"I may not be able to get back to that place," I say. "There was something about my construction that let me sneak through the gates last time. But now they know what that something is."

"Aren't you curious to find out?"

"Very," I admit. "But..."

I search for a way to describe my combination of interest and apathy. Staring at the egg rolls offers no inspiration.

"I need to think about this."

"Naturally," she is thrilled.

"I said I would think about it," I try to temper her expectations.

"And I appreciate that," she likewise tries to anchor her buoyancy, but without conviction.

Our food is cold.

I take out my list of private investigators, draw an X over the names, turn over the paper, and use the back to compose a list of my favorite haunts.

"In case you want to go someplace decent before heading back," I explain.

"Thanks."

"I would join you," I excuse myself as I write. "But I need to be free of all distractions and influences. This has to be my choice and mine alone."

"Take all the time you need," she says. "If he's in the place where I'm asking you to look for him, he's not going anywhere."

On the drive home I meditate on the notion of trying to find someone in the place where I found myself. The part of me that exists separate from Devin was found in the place where Kelly says nobody goes anywhere. She is somewhat right. They go nowhere physically. Meanwhile back on earth, where everybody goes everyplace physically, I have been staggered by the feeling of going nowhere in spirit, in spite of my choices.

Sitting alone in my empty condominium does not feel much different from when I am circulating in the world. This is the most surprising part of my philanthropy. If I had any close friends in place before pursuing my foundation, maybe one of them would have warned me about the pitfalls of charity. They would describe the frustration of suspecting what I do will never be enough, the bitterness of when a beneficiary is ungrateful, the heartbreak of saying no to so many requests, the guilt of enjoying the ability to say no. I like to think losing much of the anonymity I cultivated heightened every disappointment, gossip travels faster than non-disclosure agreements, but my charitable stupor runs deeper than keeping my name off the walls can reach. I assumed contributing to large-scale, structural needs would lead to change, and still believe it most days, but at times I feel I may accomplish more by walking around the discount shopping center handing out hundred dollar bills.

Other times I want to tell those who are struggling to hang on, better days are coming in a place where days do not exist. I know. I have been there.

Or so I think.

I never tell them because I wonder if afterlives may vary, or mine was not an afterlife, but some kind of shared-mind experience with Devin, like Kelly mentioned. And even if it was what it seemed to be, days to come are not worth the price of present days. There are so many to fill, and so much of the afterlife appears to depend on what happens in this one.

Plus I can think of nothing else I would rather spend Devin's money on.

I was in that place where they thought I was done with my body for a month's worth of days on earth, between the day we launched the videogame and the day we sold the company, so I use one month as the baseline for deciding on how long I should request to be put under if I decide to go.

When I decide to go.

Of course I am going.

There is no way I am not going, unless the landlords of the afterworld have changed the locks.

Or my creators deny me.

# Chapter Two

When I call Kelly to plan a trip to the afterworld, she celebrates by crying for ten seconds, recovering for another ten, then gets down to the business of how long the travel package should last. I am about to suggest my one-month yardstick when she opens the bidding at one day.

"All you need to do is see if Dad is there," she justifies her proposal. "In and out."

I pace about the living room of my condo, the lack of furniture allowing for plenty of room to move, and try to explain into the phone how time evaporates on the other side, how I cannot estimate how much of it elapsed because days are not twenty-four hours, they are as long as you need them to be, so they are not really days, and hours are not hours for that matter, so I am unable to line up my time spent away from earth alongside the one month that passed while I was gone and arrive at any sort of formula or exchange rate.

"Maybe one day away would seem like the same amount of time as my last visit, maybe not. It might not even be enough to finish the conversation I'm sure I'll end up having with the manager when and if I get there."

"The manager?" her voice gawks.

"It's not what you think," I let her down. "They have a massive bureaucracy thick with layers. If there is a god, you need to know someone to get an appointment."

"I would think you're someone over there. Or will be after you make a return trip. How often does that happen?"

"It still may not."

"But if it does..." she soaks in a pause.

I listen to the silence on her end and consider how I can somehow hear it across the one hundred miles that separate us. I stop pacing and start concocting similarities between how my space and her space are connected by invisible waves, and how the before and afterlife may be connected.

"There are no celebrities in the afterlife," I regroup and take another slow lap around the living room.

"You said you have to know someone to get to the top floor."

"That was a figure of speech. I don't know how it actually works."

She breathes as though she is trying to grow taller.

"Or you don't want to tell me," she accuses.

"I told you how time works there."

"Yeah. Thank you for that. But you can't see time. There's nothing to see. It's time."

"I've said too much already," I embellish my point. "As much as I tease the management, I also assured them I wouldn't violate their trust."

"Okay, well, then I guess there's nothing else to talk about. Let me know if the cloners buy your pitch, and I'll give you a ride to the lab."

"Kelly…"

"What?"

"Your idea to run with my story, the truth, or something close to it, is genius. It's what got me to thinking maybe we can pull this off."

"Thank you," she settles down.

"Once you finally got around to telling me."

She laughs and static bursts across the connection between us for a second.

"So," I signal a return to where we were headed before the static hit, "do you have any advice as far as the tone is concerned? My delivery?"

"You were built to promote yourself. You don't need my help."

"You know them better than I do," I remind her. "I met those two stiffs at the hospital for five minutes when you tried to re-create the ending of The Wizard of Oz."

"Those two stiffs will probably be the ones you have to pitch. They'll certainly be part of the team. It's a small, closed circle of people working there."

"How do I break though it?"

From what I can hear, she may be doing some pacing of her own now.

"When Gina joked about them being clones," she says, "it was funny because it's true. Or seems to be. They're like failed clones that aren't enough like real people, so they keep them working for the company instead of letting them out into the world."

"I won't bother appealing to their emotions, then."

"There's nothing to appeal to."

"And asking for only one day feeds into that overly logical feel of theirs?"

"Sure," she wavers. "It would give them answers right away."

"You too."

I imagine her stopping and looking at the floor.

"My daddy issues aside," she eases into her reason. "They're going to want the same answers I do, the same answers everyone wants."

"Even cold, calculating corporate drones?"

"Everyone."

"I suppose so."

"And those cold, calculating corporate drones get to hear those answers," she says. "Unlike me."

We ride another pause a hundred miles wide and five seconds long.

"Not if I don't tell them anything."

I am certain I can hear her smile.

"You sneaky clone you," she adds to the sound of her smile.

I try to make what I can hear of it even bigger.

"I wouldn't think of telling them any more than I would tell you."

"Did I say sneaky?" she says, and from the sound of it, I have succeeded in broadening her smile. "I meant honorable and dignified. What are you going to tell them when you return?"

I lower myself into the futon facing the wall where I gather most people would hang a television screen.

"I'll tell them it was an entirely different experience this time, unlike anything that happened the first time, which means it was an elaborate dream, nothing more."

"They won't be satisfied."

"But they'll believe it."

"You sure?"

"It's everyone's favorite default explanation. You and Jalen and Gina tried to convince me in the hospital I was dreaming. When in doubt, it was all a dream."

"Maybe you should ask for more than one day."

We split the difference between a day and a month, deciding on two weeks, with the idea we can settle for one.

If we reach that point in negotiations.

First I have to convince the company I am worth haggling with.

"I want to tell you a story of death," I address the drones. "But before I do that, I want to thank you for giving me life. I wouldn't have the opportunity to share my story if not for the gift of life your company granted me."

As Kelly predicted, the man and woman who were at the hospital when I was revived are seated across from me in a conference room. They may have personalities, but appear to take pride in hiding them, the light gray walls and dark gray carpeting a reflection of their efforts. They are joined by another eerie, silent man who is there to take the minutes of our meeting.

"Life precedes death," says the woman to the man.

"Duly noted," the main man nods.

He turns to the man typing on the keyboard taking minutes.

"Did you get that?" he asks him.

"Life before death," the minutes man answers. "Check."

They all stare at me. The man on the minutes returns to his tapping.

"I never would have guessed from our brief interaction at the hospital that you have such a sharp sense of humor," I compliment them.

"Which one of us are you addressing?" the woman asks.

"Both of you."

"Don't you think Donnie is funny?" the man gestures toward the typist.

"He plays off you really well," I acknowledge. "You're a good team."

"He's the funniest individual at the company," the woman says.

Donnie remains buried in minutes, oblivious to any praise.

"No egos here," I note. "How refreshing."

"Well, Mr. Orr—" the man interrupts himself. "Do you go by Mr. Orr?"

"Everyone thinks that's who I am."

"No secrets between us," he says.

"Also very refreshing," I keep holding up the sunny side.

"Now that we've gotten to know each other a bit," the woman picks up the trail the man was forging. "What is it exactly you want to tell us? You mentioned something about death."

"Yes," I swap the sunny side for a more sincere tone. "I did."

"And what is it you'd like to tell us about death today?" the man asks.

"Besides that life comes before it," Donne pitches in.

"See?" the woman gestures his way. "Always on."

"Indeed," I play along. "Good one, Donnie."

He is already back to tapping.

I return to my task as well.

"I've been there," I cast aside their distractions. "That's what I'd like to tell you about death today."

I finally seem to have their attention.

"At least I think I have," I follow up. "It sure seemed like it."

I had planned on qualifying my statement to help set up the need for a return trip, but I did not plan on it sounding so meek. Their stares are much more withering than I anticipated.

"And this was while you were in hibernation with us?" the man asks.

"Yes," I confirm. "After Devin's team ushered you out of the hospital room when they realized their mock dream scheme didn't work, I dropped some knowledge on them that only someone hanging out with the dead could know."

"Knowledge you obtained while under our care?" the woman wants to know.

Another angle I had not expected. They are full of surprises.

"Are you concerned about proprietary rights?" I ask.

"We're trying to understand what you're telling us," says the man.

"Legal ground is a safe space for us," adds the woman.

"It's how we process most information," the man completes their explanation.

"Let's back up," the woman offers. "So...you came by that information through meetings with dead people. Whoa."

"Unbelievable," the man mirrors her deadpan.

"Is that better?" the woman asks.

It will have to do.

"Yes," I answer both of her queries at once. "Some dead people filled me in on some living people."

"What did they fill you in on?" the man asks.

"You're doing it again," I sigh. "Aren't you at all interested in what it was like? What it looked like? Felt like? What the weather was like? How old or young the people decided to be?"

"I imagine the weather is very nice," she says.

"I imagine they all decide to be young," he says.

"That seemed to be the case for the most part," I say.

"You're not certain?" she asks.

"That's why I'm here. It was such a vivid experience. So real. So beautiful. But it scared me to think about what it was, what it might be, so I tried to put it behind me for a while. But that's not possible. Those ghosts haunt me, as ghosts will do. At the same time, though, I'm losing touch with them, with what happened, which is leading to confusion. I want clarity. I need answers. Since Devin retired, he hasn't needed me as much as he thought he would, so what narrow purpose I did have is gone, leaving me with more time than ever to wonder what happened. My hope is that the search for clarity and for answers will provide me with a new purpose."

"You want us to put you under again," he says.

"That's right."

"For research purposes," she says.

"Uh huh."

"To further investigate...heaven? The hereafter? What do you prefer to call it?" he asks.

"I tend to go with afterlife."

The man and the woman look at each other.

"I can't recall a meeting quite like this one. Can you?" she asks him.

"I cannot," he answers her.

Donnie spasms and reaches into his back pocket for a cell phone.

He pulls it out, reads a text, then slides the phone back into his pocket.

Without acknowledging any of us, he folds his laptop and exits the conference room.

The man and woman are not surprised. They watch him go as if he bid them a pleasant good bye.

The three of us to sit together in silence.

The man and woman are comfortable with it, but when we reach the ten second mark, I break it up.

"If we have a conversation and Donnie doesn't record it, did it really happen?"

"No," the woman says.

I surrender to the quiet and try to find the kind of comfort they have in it, but struggle.

The door opens soon after my search begins.

A woman enters dressed for a sunny day of window shopping and brunch in a seaside hamlet.

"You too," she barks at the man and woman.

They rise and leave without a word.

"Leave the door open," she further orders them before approaching me with hand extended.

Her light scarf, light wrap, and light dress fill the air around her, making it appear as though she is floating in my direction. When she stops, everything falls into an unveiling. She must not undress so much as unwrap.

"Mr. Orr," the command in her voice remains, in vivid contrast to her wardrobe and movements.

"Hello," I feel as though I would lose my hand if I refuse to shake hers.

"What a pleasant surprise this meeting turned out to be," her voice and the word 'pleasant' build on the unlikely pairing of her appearance and her tone, which remains the same whether giving orders or commendations.

"Trisha Miter," she stops shaking my hand but keeps clutching it. "This is my company."

"A pleasure to meet you."

"We've met before but you were designed to forget it ever happened. Let's go to my office."

She leaves in her hurricane of silk and chiffon.

I scramble to catch up. I follow her down the hall, feeling as though I may need to wave my arms in front of me to part the churn of fabric and mood. When she makes an abrupt turn into her office, the hallway seems to settle, a stiff breeze having passed, leaving behind a sober calm.

Her office completes the cycle of polarities, a crack of sunlight in the cloudy skies that cover the rest of the building. It looks like one of the galleries in the seaside hamlet she is dressed for. Sculptures utilizing all manner of rocks, minerals, and metals are scattered throughout the space, large pieces on the floor, smaller works on every available tabletop. Every color appears to be represented several times in various shades across the prints on the walls, the upholstery on the furniture, even the food in the bowls and baskets, some of which might be part of the sculpture collection.

She is already seated on a couch in the lounge area across the room from her desk. She directs me to close the door. If it was Halloween, I would assume this is an elaborate costume, the ruthless CEO dressed as a wellness guru, a winking attempt at self-awareness for the benefit of her otherwise tormented workforce.

"I'm not a hypocrite," she reads my mind while gesturing for me to take a seat on the couch that meets hers at a ninety-degree angle in the configuration. "The rest of the tech bros in this industry, the ones seducing their employees with pasta bars and ping pong to stay in the office all the time, they're the hypocrites."

I sit where I am told as she continues.

"I'm encouraging my employees to have a life, to see the office building for what it really is. It's my life, not theirs."

"Are your employees really capable of that?"

She laughs.

"Not that I've met many of them," I qualify.

"No," she takes a breath. "You're right. I have a type. Do you think that type would be happy with dart boards and kegs of beer?"

"Probably not."

She reaches out to a copper and aluminum sculpture on the coffee table catty corner from us. With a flick of her finger, the medallion in the center spins, alternating between the sun on one side and moon on the other, each wearing a wise smirk, while the same mechanism makes metal waves around the base where big fish jump after little fish day and night.

"This way they have a chance to build a life of their own," she watches the sculpture spin.

"I suspect their homes look very much like the rest of this building," I say. "Like Devin. His house looks like an extension of his office."

"Ah, Devin. Speaking of tech bros. Is he letting you crash at his place?"

"I have a place of my own."

"He should never have ordered you if he had even the slightest inkling he might sell the company. Very short-sighted and selfish."

"The living arrangements are my choice. I moved someplace where no one would know who he is. Only two hours away, but it might as well be two time zones."

"And you've been stewing in thoughts of life after death."

"I have."

"Have you shared any of these thoughts with Devin?"

"I have not."

"Just as well. I don't know what he would contribute. Hardly a deep thinker."

"Strong work ethic," I put up a mild defense.

"That's not what this situation requires."

She halts the gears on the sculpture, then ignites it again as she resumes talking.

"You truly believe our technology found a workaround to the afterworld."

"I do."

"Like a fake ID that gets you into heaven's gate."

"Why die when you can clone your way in?"

"You're a born salesman," she praises my slogan. "Literally."

We stare at one another. I consider saying 'Thanks, Mom.'

"If we do this," she saves me from myself. "It's not going to be a personal journey."

"I figured as much."

"I want to know exactly what happens."

"Of course."

"And if your experience confirms what happened last time, we work together."

"Doing what?"

"We'll worry about that if it turns out we really have engineered the greatest unintended consequence in human history."

The words 'unintended' and 'human' stick to me.

"Are there others?" I ask.

She watches the sun and moon trade places and the waves rise and fall and the fish swim and refrains from fiddling with them this time.

"You're our first," she keeps staring at the machinery. "We usually deal in plants and animals."

"Am I legal?"

"You're *our* first, but not *the* first."

"So there was an approval process."

She looks at me and decides to grin.

"I'm going to need proof," she pretends the previous fifteen seconds never happened.

I am in no position to lift anymore rocks to see what lies underneath.

"You're not going to take my word for it?"

"Consider it a compliment. You're human enough for me not to trust you."

"What does that proof look like?"

"Like my second stepfather."

"How many did you have?"

"He was the last one."

"How did he die?"

"That's for me to know, and you to find out."

She reaches for a bowl of brightly-colored candies on the side table where our couches meet.

"Skittle?" she offers.

# Chapter Three

"His name is Cam Lamp," I say to Kelly as I uncork the bottle of Cabernet I brought her for letting me stay at her house the night before she is due to drive me to the lab.

"It is?" she watches me from one the barstools at the kitchen counter.

"I know," I pour her a glass. "He should really go with the full name. Cameron Lamp sounds much better."

"Is that all you need to look for him?" she asks. "Just his name?"

"Nope," I hand her the glass across the counter and remain standing in the kitchen.

"Oh, come on," she accepts my donation but wants more than wine. "What does sharing intel on Cam Lamp even have to do with the afterworld?"

"Nothing," I grin and come out of the kitchen to join her on the other side. "I just like to tease you."

"I'm curious, not nosy."

"What's the difference?"

"Knowledge, not gossip."

"Like my buddy Nita," I hop on the barstool next to hers.

"Who?"

"My favorite server at my favorite restaurant," I reach for an M & M from the bowl she keeps on the counter. "Since I don't know Mr. Lamp personally, I asked Ms. Miter where he would spend his time if he could hang out anywhere he wanted. What kinds of places, if not specific ones."

"And where's that?" she asks.

I pop the candy in my mouth and draw an imaginary line between us on the countertop with my finger.

"It was worth a shot," she takes a sip. "If only you could drink tonight then maybe I'd get more out of you."

"Devin wasn't much of a drinker," I have a vision, or lack thereof. "I have no memories of him being drunk."

"I can't help but indulge," she apologizes. "I'm nervous."

"That's fine. I feel like I brought the perfect gift."

"This reminds me of the lead-up up to the launch, when we were planning on putting you under the first time. We were supposed to watch you like hawks to make sure you didn't drink for twenty-four hours before the shot. One sip and we were sunk."

I draw imaginary circles on my side of the imaginary line.

"If Devin did drink maybe his memory bank would be more interesting," I imagine.

"So are you going to look for this Lamp guy?"

"Are you kidding? I want nothing to do with Trisha Miter. I'm pretty sure she had a knife tucked somewhere under all that cloth. Maybe more than one."

"You're not at all curious?"

"She seemed really proud of knowing how he died."

"You could look him up and not tell her. You already know what you're going to say when you get back, anyway."

"Honestly, she's the least of my concerns."

"Are you nervous, too?" she spots an opportunity to tease me back.

"It's all about the other side now," I tempt the possibility of talking more about something I have been sitting on for a while. "I've started to think they won't let me in now that they know I'm out there. I'm going to wake up in two weeks and the only thing I'll remember is the anesthesiologist asking me to count backwards from ten. Like I had a colonoscopy."

"That would be a long colonoscopy."

"Even if I do get in, they were really irritated with me last time. I was a bug in their system."

"Trisha's company is the bug," Kelly assures me while trying not to look too enchanted by my loosening lips regarding the afterlife. "You were just the messenger."

"And I'm using her company to gain access again. They might not be pleased. Maybe they let me in only to do something spiteful."

"What's the worst they could do?"

"Before Devin went scuba diving, when we all still thought I had been put out of commission rather than put on ice, we negotiated a mulligan."

"Like in golf?"

"Yes."

"Huh."

"Can I have a glass of water?" I rise to head back into the kitchen. "I'll serve myself."

"Sure," she processes the new information I have fed her about life after death. "Uh, okay. Glasses are in the cupboard over the toaster. Water dispenser is in the freezer door."

"Thanks," I go about my business, relieved to be sharing, wondering if I should be, and bracing myself for the next question.

"What exactly is a mulligan in golf?" she asks.

I sip and smile.

"It's a do-over," I remain standing in the kitchen.

"Oh my," she cracks the analogy. "You were going to come back as someone else?"

"Yup," I roll with the confessional, my dread over tomorrow driving me deeper into sharing. "From the beginning, though. Not a takeover. Not *Invasion of the Body Snatchers* or *Freaky Friday*. None of that. It was going to be from birth."

"Wow," Kelly looks as though that may be her last word before taking a vow of silence. "You were going to be reborn. Actually born again."

"Well, if you count the way I came into the world as being born."

"Re-created?" she tries another verb.

"Then Devin showed up," I remind her of the twist.

"And the deal was off."

"They said if we tried the mulligan and I was whisked back here while my new self was in someone's womb somewhere else, it could be catastrophic."

"How so?"

"They didn't say exactly, just that pretty much every path it carved wouldn't lead anywhere good."

"Thank God Devin showed up when he did."

"That's your takeaway?" I take a water break.

"Think of what might have happened if he showed up right after they gave you the mulligan."

"In other words, I should be grateful you killed him when you did."

"When 'they' killed him," she corrects me. "Maybe 'we'. Definitely not 'I.'"

She is bothered by the memory, but how much is hard to quantify.

"I've always assumed you were the third-most enthusiastic person in the boat when Jalen and Gina decided to run out the clock on him."

Kelly gulps a larger swig than usual and emerges indifferent to that day on the boat and refocused on my afterlife travel log.

"You could have come back as one of those adults with a fetish for being a baby."

"Management seemed a lot more concerned about the actual baby."

"That's not right," she suppresses a hiccup. "What about you? Trying to run a charity while hiding your cravings for warm milk and strained carrots."

I appreciate that the memory must be traumatizing, so I embrace the diversion she is crafting. Besides, it sounds fun.

"Clients hearing my diaper rustle when I sit down," I join in.

"All the money you would blow on adult-sized playpens and changing tables."

"Hiring women to change me."

"If anyone found out, you'd be ruined."

"All that good work, flushed down the toilet."

"No!" she wields her glass like a weapon and extends her index finger along its side.

"No?"

"Yes, your work would be finished, but not down the toilet. Because you'd be wearing diapers."

"You win," I raise my glass. "Which is only fair, since you started it."

"They wouldn't do that to you," she moves beyond jokes and metaphors. "It's inhumane."

"Thank you for using the word 'inhumane.'"

"It's true."

"It's got the word 'human' in it. I never take that for granted when it happens."

My sincerity catches up with hers faster than she expected.

"I can't help but feel I'm pushing my luck," I take advantage of her need to regroup. "I should never have been there in the first place, and now I'm going back."

She sips her wine and brews the best assurance she can on short notice.

"It sounds like not getting in is really all you have to worry about. And that wouldn't be the worst thing. You won't have to lie to anyone."

"I'd have to disappoint you."

"It would be a relief," she studies the invisible circles I drew on the counter. "If you get in, you're going to find him. I'm sure. And I'm not sure I'm ready to face that."

Before I knew what I was, when my identity was strictly Devin, I would dread the night before a business trip. In addition to the worries over what might go wrong, there was a feeling of impending displacement, of existing only to conduct business, which of course turned out to be true. I was built for business. Whatever trip loomed the next morning had little to do with those feelings.

So as Kelly and I take a break from each other, not ready to say good night, but unable to talk anymore about where she is taking me tomorrow, I hold up what I am feeling tonight against what I felt before I was anything other than Devin. I discover there is no difference. Business is business.

We retreat to separate sides of her living room and into our phones. I send a text to Everything reminding him to set up an out-of-office reply for all inquiries over the next two weeks. He writes back within a minute to say he has, and this is the second time he has told me. To quote him: "I did right away when asked and told you first time."

Since I have his attention, I ask him what he has planned for his time off.

"Nothing."

I tell him he should take a trip.

"Where?"

I ask if there is any place he has dreamed of visiting.

"No."

Not even someplace obvious like Disneyland or Italy?

"Maybe Legoland."

I encourage him to follow through on that uncertain dream, and send him the names of all the other amusement parks and zoos in the San Diego area, which may overwhelm him, because he stops texting.

I try to imagine him researching the parks, but all I can conjure up is him playing video games or watching prank videos.

I compose an apology, claiming I never meant to apply any pressure, but delete it. Instead I write a text to send in case I return with no connection to my current self, or do not return at all. I tell him he has been a good attorney, an ideal partner, and that Kelly will be a good boss, probably better than me.

I ask Kelly if she has pen and paper. She directs me to one of the top drawers in the kitchen, she cannot remember which one exactly. Among the rubble inside the second drawer that I check, I find a pen from our old company and a pad of paper from a real estate agent. I write a sentence directing Everything to transfer my assets to Kelly in the event of my physical or mental disappearance, and then I take a picture of what I have written.

Kelly asks what I am doing.

I show her and tell her to send the picture and the text if necessary.

She looks more overwhelmed than Everything must have looked when I sent him the list of San Diego attractions.

"You'll be fine," I say.

"People might get suspicious," she frets.

"Keep your job, pick foundation projects when you have the time, and don't spend any of that money on yourself. Nobody can touch you."

She is not convinced.

"Please come back," she says.

"That's the plan."

I think she moves in for a hug a split second before I do. My hunch is confirmed when she takes longer to let go.

A dozen footsteps later we stand in front of our bedroom doors and say good night.

We say little else leading up to our trip to the lab.

Good morning in her kitchen for breakfast, and good bye in her car when she drops me off.

We have a couple of other exchanges, some of them quite clever I imagine, but they fail to impress as much as a simple good night, good morning, and good bye. My mind is too busy with what comes next.

The weather offers no distractions. The sky is clear and the air is still. I am the only one approaching the front doors of the building, the only one in the lobby other than the woman behind the front desk who checks me in, the only one in the elevator, and the only one in the hallway leading to the room where my departure is scheduled.

Behind the door is another conference room, rather than a lab.

"The lab comes later," Trisha announces from the head of the table.

She is draped in her customary layers of crepe, the beige and white neutrality of the main articles punctuated by vibrant scarves of violet and fuchsia.

"First we need to verify a few things," she gestures for me to sit at the table on the side closest to the door.

On the other side of her sits Donnie, laptop open, ready to record the minutes.

I nod at him and take my seat.

"What's my stepfather's name?" she asks.

"Cameron Lamp."

"Cam."

"I still don't get that."

"I don't either," she confides. "Never did. What have you learned about his death?"

"That he died on a cruise ship to Mexico with your mother."

"How?"

"That's as far as the web took me."

"I'll give you a little more to go on. Maybe it'll help your investigation."

"Every little bit does."

"He choked on a piece of cake."

"Huh," I think it over. "I suppose there are worse things to choke on."

"Once the choking starts I don't think it matters much how you got there. Do you remember the other things I've told you?"

"I do."

"Where does he like to hang out?"

"High school football games."

"And?"

"Aquariums."

"How would I describe him to friends who had yet to meet him?"

"He always looks like he's peering through a pair of binoculars."

"True or false," she leans back, but not far enough to press against the back of the chair. "It's a good idea to mention my name when talking to him."

"False."

"Who is the best person to use when trying to get information out of him?"

"His son."

"Why is that?"

"All the feelings. Equal parts joy and regret."

"How come?"

"They had not spoken in five years when he died."

She at last leans the rest of the way back, as though expecting the chair to recline.

"How are you feeling?" she asks.

"Different this time," I say. "There are expectations."

"Is that why you're nervous?"

"So it shows."

"Whose expectations make you nervous? Mine? Or your own?"

"My own."

"Explain."

"Things took me by surprise before. Even getting there. I was ambushed. Now I know."

"Or you think you know."

"That's right."

"All you're giving me is the definition of expectations. I was hoping for a more specific reason."

"Ask me a more guiding question."

"What scares you?"

"That none of it was real."

"I've heard you say that before. Why does it matter?"

"Because then I won't be as special as I thought I was."

She smiles.

"Thank you," she says before thinking of something that curdles her grin. "Dammit. Donnie? I just remembered."

"What can I do for you, Ms. Miter?" he stops typing.

"I left my key card to the lab in my office. Can you go fetch it?"

"Absolutely," he springs into action and walks around the table behind her, then behind me to reach the door.

He never reaches it.

Instead he gathers me into a headlock and spins my chair to face Trisha. She unveils a syringe from the flows of her blouse, or maybe from her wrap. It is difficult to tell where one ends and the other begins.

My first instinct is to resist, but unlike backstage at the video game launch, I yield.

"Sorry," Trisha says, wheeling forward in her chair and drawing the needle toward my neck. "We thought it best to simulate the circumstances of the first time as much as possible."

"Good idea," I admit before my ability to speak is poked away.

"We all want it to be real," she assures me while draining the syringe of its contents.

I hear the door open and try to see who enters, but am already unable to move. Trisha withdraws the needle and Donnie lowers me onto the floor. A circle forms around us made of people dressed in lab coats and surgical masks, looking down at me. I visualize giving them all a thumbs up, like an astronaut through the window of a rocket ship during the last digits of the countdown.

# Chapter Four

The cubicle is empty again on arrival.

I am sitting in a chair by myself next to an unoccupied desk.

I stand up to see if the rest of the office is how I remember it, which it is, and place this cubicle on my recollection of the grid to see if it belongs to Melt, which it does not. Besides, he would already be here slapping my shoulder and opening his arms for a possible hug. The policy must be to let a new resident sit alone for a minute before approaching them, and I must be a new resident to the worker in this cubicle.

I am relieved to have made it this far, but assume the word is out and the wheels are in motion.

An unfamiliar woman enters who would fit right in with the gray labor pool at Trisha's company, except for the fact this woman is smiling.

"Hello, Mr. Orr."

"Hello."

"We'll get started in a moment," she sits down at her desk.

"Okay.

I wonder if she means the usual spiel, or whatever is in store for me if word traveled fast enough for someone to get in her ear before our meeting.

"Out of curiosity..." she settles in with a conspiratorial grin.

"Yes?"

"Who was your escort?"

"My escort?"

"Was it a grandparent?" she reminds me of the step I leapfrogged again. "I'll bet it was a grandparent."

"Yes," I capitalize on her wager. "My grandfather guided me into the light."

"How sweet."

"My dear old grandpa and his side piece, Angela."

She rears back.

"Can't say I've heard that one before," she maintains most of her smile.

"Their love knows no bounds."

"I see..." she scans her desk for the best way to shift into the orientation.

Melt bursts into the opening of the cubicle before she begins.

"You're back!" he spreads his arms.

"Hello, Melt," I remain seated.

"You're back?" my orientation facilitator, if that is her job title, stares at me.

"You probably haven't heard that before, either."

She cannot muster a response.

The manager appears in the opening as Melt drifts toward me with open arms.

"My office," the manager beckons with his index finger.

"Just in time," I stand as Melt stops, drops his arms, and turns to catch up with his boss.

"Nice to meet you," I tell the woman on my way out of her space.

Halfway to the manager's office, we pass what I think may be Melt's cubicle. My suspicion is confirmed when the manager shoves him into it.

"Good to see you again, Melt," I say as I pass by.

"You too," he murmurs in a manner that makes it easy to imagine how forlorn he looks.

When we reach the manager's office, he holds open the door for me. I thank him and take the first available seat on the couch next to the threshold.

"I was afraid of this," he says as the door closes behind him on his way across the room.

"Can you blame me?"

He sighs and sinks into the chair behind his desk.

"How did you convince them to put you under again?"

"I told them what happened, and that I wanted to double check to see if it was true."

"You told them?" he lurches forward.

"Yes, but that was just a hook. I'm going to tell them the experiences don't match."

"So what's the purpose your visit?"

"I'm here for a friend."

"Dead or alive?"

"Alive."

He stares at me while considering the implications.

"Does this friend of yours know you're here?"

I wait as long as I can before answering.

"It was her idea."

He collapses in a heap, his top half splayed on the desk, the lower half piled onto the chair.

"She wants to know if her father is dead," I offer my defense.

The manager looks more distraught than he or Melt looked the first time I met them.

"How did she even get it in her head that it was possible to check?" he seems to ask anyone who will listen, even though I am the only one in the room with him.

"She was part of the team from Devin's company that tried to screw him over, screw us over."

"The people you were supposed to freak out by sharing knowledge only Devin could know?"

"The same."

"So much for that idea."

"It worked. They were freaked out. Terribly. But one of them had this thing happen with her dad, and she got to thinking about that other thing that happened with her boss. About a year passed before it all came together."

"I don't care if ten years passed. You're making the mistakes of your creators ten times worse."

"Plenty of people on earth have their suspicions."

"But they didn't have proof. Until now."

"It's only one person."

"I know enough about the human race to know it's not going to stop with just one person."

"I'll keep it under wraps. Believe me. You think I want that kind of attention?"

He stares at the ceiling, or perhaps something above it.

"What is her father's name?" he asks with a pushy calm.

I realize something.

"Her last name is Arias."

He realizes what I have realized.

"You don't know his first name?"

"Oddly enough, it never came up."

He exerts more effort in maintaining his serenity.

"Great planning," he breathes.

"We had big questions we were grappling with," I reach for an excuse.

"People take trips all the time that force them to grapple with big questions. But they remember to bring their ticket to the airport."

"I have memories of Devin meeting him. I guess Kelly assumed I also remembered his name."

"Did her father invest any money in Devin's company?"

"No."

"Did Devin invest any money in her father?"

"No."

"Then why would she think Devin would remember his name?"

"His name is Arias, he's in multinational banking, he was on a business trip to Croatia when he disappeared. That should be enough."

"Should it?"

"I would think."

"You would think," he turns it into a pejorative as he reaches for the device on his desk and feeds it the information.

I reach for the door and crack it open while I wait.

He glares at me.

"Just seeing if Melt has his ear pressed to it," I say and shut it.

He appreciates the effort and relents a bit.

"Well," he narrates his navigation. "I have an international banker named Arias who joined us during a trip, but it wasn't to Croatia."

"Really?"

"And it wasn't for business."

"Huh."

He puts down the device and looks at me.

"And you trust this man's daughter not to pull the thread that's now hanging from the fabric of the universe?"

"She didn't know he was lying."

"You'd better be sure."

"Where was he?" I bypass his fussing. "And what was he doing there?"

"Why don't you ask him?"

"Really?"

"He already accepted your request."

A rush of anxiety spreads to the tip of every nerve in my body.

"That was fast," I steady my voice.

"I sent it while I was researching him."

The anxiety retreats from my nerve endings and crumples into a ball that sinks into my stomach.

"Maybe it's not him," I half hope.

"He wouldn't have responded."

"Maybe it's another globe-trotting guy named Arias who's really into video games, recognized my name, and would like to meet me."

"What's going on?"

"Technically I don't even need to visit him. I already have confirmation he's here."

"Why the cold feet?"

"I'm dead. It's a side effect."

"You've come this far."

"What about you? Why the sudden encouragement?"

"If I have to cover for you creeping around the afterlife, I want you to finish what you started."

"Fair enough."

"You owe your friend that much."

"This is a very noble side of you."

"Plus it keeps you out of my sight."

"You couldn't ride your good side for even a few more seconds?"

"Her father has an incredible spread overlooking the ocean," he explains as if it justifies all past and future insults.

"In this market?"

I take a hearty breath and visualize Kelly's father in a five-bedroom, eight-bath on the shores of south Orange County, or maybe the Mediterranean. He was a world traveler, after all.

"Before you go..." the manager flags down my train of thought.

"Yes?" I compete with his brand of irritation.

"Remember you're Devin to him. No big reveals about the cloning."

"I figured. Can I start visualizing now?"

"Also..."

I stifle a grunt.

"...Checking on Mr. Arias isn't going to take long. I hope you weren't planning on meeting up with your old friends. I can't have it, not with Devin lurking around."

"But they got the announcement that I arrived. Doesn't someone need to explain the situation?"

"Nice try. Announcements aren't released until after orientation now. We changed the policy thanks to you."

"That must slow things down."

"There is no slow or fast here."

"Then why did you have announcements go out early in the first place?"

He appears to quiver, as though his human form may be concealing a demon he is about to unleash. He uses the business at hand to settle down.

"Keep a low profile," he implores. "If you visit any of your dead friends, I'll know."

"You can do that?"

"Like a bell around your neck."

"You're bluffing."

"You can find out. Or you can come up with some sequels to jet-skiing with dolphins. Doesn't that sound like more fun? Maybe play rugby with kangaroos, or mountain bike with sasquatch."

"Is that the plural of sasquatch? Like fish and fish? Or do you mean one sasquatch on a bike?"

"It'll make it easier to run interference for you," he ignores my question.

"Are sasquatch real?" I try another one.

"Wouldn't know. Not our department."

"Do animals have their own afterlife?"

"I thought you were ready to get going."

"It's a conversation I had with Jane."

"I don't know," he strains. "I have one job. I am a cog in this vast, complex machine. Now, please focus on Arias and the ocean and the eyesore he carved into the hills above it."

"Is it that ugly?"

"Find out!"

"Okay, okay," I take a deep breath and lean back on the couch. "Geesh."

He is correct.

Not about the house, which is lovely.

He said the mission is likely not to take long, which is true, and I failed to reply with any truth of my own, which is that I am overwhelmed by the thought of coming up with ways to fill the days, or hours, or whatever void takes the place of time, especially now that visiting old friends is not viable. I wish I was scheduled for two days in the lab rather than two weeks. An abbreviated stay would still give everyone everything they want. Kelly would know her dad is dead, and Trisha would know what I tell her. I was too caught up in negotiating timelines to consider what forms those lines may draw. I am surprised at how much the afterlife continued to feel like an abstraction even after a round trip. Now that I am back, preparing for events rather than reacting to them, the prospect of eternity, even for two weeks, is menacing.

The Arias compound is a reflection of my fears. The wraparound stone-paved porch, the portico entry, dormer windows, and infinity pool meandering beneath a trellis dripping with wisteria offer a glimpse of heaven until a longer look lingers. There is no math to reach for, no form of measurement to fall back on that may predict the moment when paradise becomes a trap.

I am surprised to see the house is part of a community, a roomy cluster of four homes, all equal in splendor, with whitewater views of the waves. Two rest along the ridgeline, with the other two a short walk up the hill behind them. I sense Mr. Arias inhabits one of the two closest to the shore, as that is the direction I find myself walking. He indeed appears on the stone porch in the space in front of me.

"Mr. Orr," he waves me up the two steps leading to him.

"Mr. Arias," I shake his hand.

"I don't know what to say first," he says. "That I'm sorry to hear of your arrival, or that I'm grateful you wanted to meet with me."

"Us young folks have to stick together here."

"Real young folks," he leads me to the patio furniture by the pool. "Not these old people pretending to be young."

"Frauds," I lower myself into a wicker love seat with a plush cushion. "One and all."

"Con artists," he sits across the coffee table from me. "The lot of them."

I breathe in the ocean air, listen to the surf below us and the seep of the infinity pool beside us, and exhale with a satisfied gaze at the purple wisteria blossoms dangling from the pergola surrounding the perimeter.

"Can I get you something to drink?" he asks.

"I think I'm good."

"Are you sure?" he sounds as though there is something about the process I should see.

"Iced tea with lemon," I give him permission to show me.

"Something in a can, perhaps."

"Okay," I play along. "Seltzer water."

"Lemon flavor?"

"Sure."

He claps his hands twice and I hear a rustling behind me. I turn to see a red ruffed lemur swinging from the wisteria vines and pergola slats with my can of seltzer clutched in one foot and a can of Tsingtao beer in the other. When he draws near, he flings the cans in the air, performs a flip, sticks the landing, and catches them in stride on his way toward us.

"Thank you, Rennie," Arias says as he accepts the beer.

"Thank you, sir," I nod upon delivery of my seltzer.

Rennie gallops back to the pergola and leaps onto the vines for his swing back to wherever he came from.

Arias shakes the can even more than it has been shaken in the swinging grip of Rennie the red ruffed lemur, then opens it without a single bubble bursting out.

"Welcome to the afterworld," he smiles.

"I thought maybe he was going to insist I call him Rennie."

"A talking lemur?" he scoffs.

I open my can and raise it in his direction. He reciprocates and we sip.

"Who lives in the other houses?" I ask.

"Parents, grandparents" he chuckles. "If we elder bash again, we should keep the volume down."

"How's that working out?" I assume not well.

"Fine, actually. We always got along."

"I tried to connect with my grandfather, but it didn't work out."

"Oh? How long have you been here?"

"Tough to say," I cover my tracks. "Time being what it is in these parts."

He sips in silent agreement and we take a moment to admire where we sit.

"So," he shifts in his cushion. "Why do I warrant a visit?"

"Well," I shift in kind. "As you know, your daughter worked for me."

He puts his can on the coffee table and stares at it.

"I knew it," he mutters.

"She's concerned. You were gone several weeks before I got here."

"What does it matter? It's not like you can tell her what happened."

I need a moment to resist bounding through the door he opened. I imagine slowly closing it, as if trying not to wake a sleeping baby.

"I'm curious," I say as the metaphorical latch clicks.

"Does she have any theories?"

"She thinks an Eastern European or Central Asian dictator had you bumped off."

"Because I'm such a big deal at my bank?" he lays the foundation for a confession.

"That's the story."

"Let her stick to it."

"I spent a lot of time listening to her."

"Thank you. I appreciate that."

"Is the real story that bad?"

"It's that disappointing. Or it would be to her."

"What about to you?"

He takes a sip and basks in a memory.

"The romance of a lifetime," he proclaims.

I hold a shrug with both palms raised and one arm extended toward him, signaling my interest and giving him his cue.

"Come on," I grin. "We're just two guys in the afterlife, having a beer together."

"You're not drinking beer."

"Neither are you, really."

He acknowledges our circumstances with a slight laugh, chugs the rest of his beer, slaps the empty can on the coffee table, and claps his hands three times.

A river otter emerges from the hedgerow on the other side of the pool, dives in, swims toward us, jumps onto the pavement by the patio furniture, clutches the empty can in his teeth, and runs away with it.

Arias sits back and ponders where to begin, or perhaps whether to begin.

"You want another?" I offer.

"Doesn't make any difference," he broods. "Like you said."

"I was hoping to find out what happens when you clap four times."

"Nothing. And Rennie only serves the first round."

"He's a conscientious lemur."

"I don't want to wear him out."

"You're a conscientious lemur owner."

"I try."

Any momentum he had a moment ago in debating his next move has disappeared. He lapses into a trance.

"You're going to have to tell her someday when she gets here," I prod him. "Might as well practice on me."

His stillness appears to gain purpose.

"I was bumped off," he lets me in. "But the hit wasn't ordered by any dictator."

"Oh?"

"The bank I worked for was involved with authoritarian regimes. But I was never part of that inner circle. When I found out, I was upset about working for such a place, and shared the information with my family, who apparently used it later on to concoct the story they're now telling themselves."

"You told them you were going on a business trip as part of that inner circle."

"I used it, too. Absolutely. All to cover up an affair."

He lets the uncorked confession breathe before pouring the rest.

"That's all it was. A good old-fashioned affair, complete with old flame and her enraged husband. My wife probably knows something and isn't telling the girls. Kelly didn't mention that her Mom thinks I ran off with someone?"

"No. Kelly wouldn't believe it, anyway."

"The running off part, at least."

He appears to trail off into a preview of the conversations he is doomed to have in the future before returning to ours in the present. And they say time fails to exist here.

"Remember when social media first came out?" he takes us into the past. "How fun it was to look up old friends and have them look you up?"

"Sure," I fib.

"I discovered my high school girlfriend was married to a very well-connected member of the Hong Kong elite."

"Is this the same high school Kelly ended up going to?"

"Yes."

"Figures."

"Remind me where you went to high school?"

"Sorry," I grant him that, "You were saying…"

"Fiona didn't post many pictures of her husband, maybe none as far as I can recall, but she posted lots of pictures of the perks. A sleepover with her kids on the golf course of the country club, girls night out on a rooftop bar overlooking the harbor, water skiing while a protest was inflaming the streets. That last one was a real 'let them eat cake' flex. That's when I started teasing her. We hadn't communicated much until then. Once we did, the teasing took on all kinds of forms. By the time our next high school reunion arrived, we were primed and ready. After that weekend, we agreed to meet every six months. I usually went over there. Not to Hong Kong specifically, too risky, but someplace nearby. We had a rotation between Taipei, Manila, Singapore…Bangkok."

"Is that where it happened?"

"I woke up one morning in our hotel room surrounded by three men. I couldn't describe them to you, because all I noticed was what they carried. One had a gun, another had a bone saw, and the third had a box of garbage bags. That's my last memory on earth. Either they worked quick, or my brain won't let me access what happened. Fiona remembers even less, just going to bed the night before. She was already gone by the time I was up."

"She's here?"

"We live together in this house."

"Wow. You're like two tragic figures in an epic poem."

"I guess. But I think those kinds of characters are usually condemned in the afterlife. They have a curse, like one can only live in the daytime and the other at night, or they're turned into animals that are different species, something where they can see each other but never be together."

"I just thought it sounded romantic."

"Thank you. You're welcome to stay for dinner."

"She won't mind?"

"She'll love it. We don't have any friends from our generation. Our parents and grandparents only go young when they throw their parties and we're never invited."

"That's probably for the best."

"It would be even better if we couldn't hear them."

"I think I know what you mean," I hint that we need not go any further.

"They're barely parties," he barrels through my stop sign. "Maybe a quick drink and a couple of songs before they start wife-swapping and tag-teaming."

As I suspected.

"Is Fiona home?" I ask out of fatigue rather than shock over the amount of afterlife sex being traded among the Greatest Generation.

"She's out hang gliding with pelicans."

"That sounds fun."

"I won't even call. We'll surprise her."

He stands up and faces the shore.

"We might be able to see her from here, pelicans willing."

He leads me toward the stairs that lower us onto the space between the house and land's end.

"The pelicans call the shots?" I follow up as I follow him.

"Always. It's their air space."

We stop close to the edge and scan the horizon. The waves roll in high and foamy. I expect a breeze, but there is none. People hate wind as much as they love water, wildlife, and sex.

"There," he points, and I focus on his target.

A line of pelicans three-dozen long soars four stories above the sea. Fiona hang-glides next to them, on the shoreline side of the aerial procession, so that we have an unobstructed view of her as they fly along at our eye level a hundred yards out.

"Spectacular," I narrate.

"Isn't it?" Arias agrees.

We watch a little while longer, which inspires me to speculate.

"I wonder why people don't give themselves the power to fly when they get here," I say without taking my eyes off the flight pattern. "Or superhuman strength or speed."

"Why don't you?" he answers my question with a question.

"That wouldn't be an ideal world," I gather. "That would be a different world."

We keep watching.

As they pass through our field of vision, the lead bird banks into a turn that takes the line back in our direction. When the line is midway through the turn, in a horseshoe formation, the leader dives toward the water, plummeting as though her wings no longer work, and splashes into a school of fish thrashing the smooth surface beyond the waves. Bird by bird the squadron follows suit, dive bombing the frothy feast.

"I guess that's it, then," I say.

"Not quite," Arias smiles.

Fiona makes the turn, and after the last bird completes its mission into the water, she unhooks herself from the hang glider and drops feet-first into the school with her comrades.

A howl streams out of me, half cheer and half convulsion.

"She only does that when it's a big enough school of fish," Arias beams. "That way there's enough for everyone, and they're easier to catch."

"With her bare hands?"

"Kind of," he grins. "She has a net in her pocket."

"I guess I know what's for dinner."

Arias pats me on the shoulder.

"Let's figure out the appetizers and sides," he guides us back toward the house.

"Can Rennie recommend a good bottle of wine to go with it?"

"Only if it comes in a can."

I almost ask where the hang glider goes, but I already know the answer. It disappears and is replaced by a new one, no matter how many times it has flown.

# Chapter Five

The evening is a delight, managing the rare feat of exceeding afterlife standards. The star-crossed lovers are also brilliant cooks, as it turns out, and pour wine of their own creation that pairs perfectly with the sockeye salmon Fiona caught in waters that on earth would be too far south and too warm to host such a magnificent fish. I step outside after dinner not so much for fresh air, but to see how my hosts have designed the night sky. They have gone with a full moon low on the horizon so that its reflection flickers on the water, making the ocean look more like a lake.

After taking in the view while processing the flavors of the food and wine, I turn to head back inside and enjoy more of their company. Before I reach the door I see them through the window. They have moved to the couch and are chewing on each other like a pair of teenagers who are not sure how long they have the house to themselves. I guess I forgot to tell them I was only stepping out for a moment.

I dare not walk past the other houses filled with gang-banging grandmas and grandpas within well-lighted windows, so I set out along the ridge, crafting a speech in my head that convinces the manager to let me visit my old friends.

My thoughts summon him before I am ready to deliver. He stands waiting in the moonlight, no Melt in sight.

"So soon?" I greet him.

"Administration knew you arrived. There was no cover to provide."

"Am I being detained?"

"Quite the contrary."

He approaches and passes me as if leading us back to the houses, but when I turn to join him, we are walking on a cramped side street in a large city. The sky is still dark, but the full moon has been carved into a waxing crescent moon that slices the night through the spaces between the buildings.

"Where is this supposed to be?" I ask.

"Who knows? The administration made it, so it's more of a movie set. None of them has ever been to a real city."

"So I'm allowed to hang out here until I go back."

"Maybe. All I know is they set up a meeting with you."

He walks us down the street toward a bar with a neon sign above the door flashing "Bar" one second, and "Open" the next, over and over.

"Another deal?" I am intrigued.

"That's my impression."

"Then where is Melt?"

"No witnesses for this one."

We reach the front of the bar and he steps to the side.

"Including me," he gestures to go inside without him. "This is strictly off the books."

The entrance is fitted with batwing doors, like an old west saloon.

"I see they like to mix genres," I note the lack of continuity.

"They wouldn't know the difference."

He nods farewell.

I nod back and push through the slatted doors, which swing behind me as I survey the interior.

They have run with a tiki theme. An awning of dried palm leaves hangs over the booths, and the handful of projections hanging out all hold colorful drinks in hurricane glasses topped with tiny plastic swords and paper umbrellas. Meanwhile the projections wear tuxedos and gowns. The dueling concepts leave the room feeling like a New Year's Eve party well past midnight.

I take a slow lap around the setting, searching for a signal, which proves to be unnecessary as I pass the third booth. A man sits in a trench coat with a fedora pulled low over his face, standing out in his effort to not stand out. I let him signal me anyway.

"Psst," he punctuates some air and pushes up the front of his fedora with a finger to the brim. "Have a seat, Doc."

"You decided on Doc," I sit across from him in the booth.

"It fits the hard-boiled atmosphere we've created," he stays in character. "It's so obviously a nickname, and people seem to go by nicknames in these kinds of murky settings."

"D.O.C. stands for Devin Orr Clone. Devin gave it to me behind my back."

"Oh," he drops the façade. "Well, Mr. Orr works, too. Anything but your first name. Nobody goes by first names in these cold-blooded games of cat and mouse."

"You like old movies."

"Never seen one. This is a popular setup for a lot of fantasies our residents act out, especially the older folks, which as you know, make up the lion's share of our population."

"I hope we stop short of how those usually end."

"I think we can make your dreams come true in other ways," he leans back with a satisfied leer and pops the collar of his trench coat.

"Okay," I lack enough information to be excited.

"Would you like something to drink?" he pauses his performance again.

"Not now. Maybe after I know what you're proposing."

"Unfettered access to anyone's simulation," he preens again. "That's our proposal."

He has my attention.

"Whether I know them or not?" I ask.

"Anyone."

"I assume it wouldn't simply be for my amusement."

"No," he admits. "But it would be pretty amusing. If that's the right word. I think it would be way more than amusing."

"What would I be doing that would leave me so much more than amused?"

"We wondered if you would return," he catches himself. "That's not the right word, either. We didn't wonder. We agonized and hoped and longed for your return. Now that we know you can travel back and forth, we would like to change some lives on earth."

"For the better?" my head fills with visions of Trisha Miter wearing seventeen layers of light fabric, surrounded by driftwood sculptures, plotting revenge on anyone more successful than her.

"You know our mission statement here," he scolds. "Why would it be any different on earth?"

"You really haven't spent any time on earth."

"Some of us don't have the good fortune to be able to world-hop. In fact, none of us do, on either side. Only you."

He snaps his fingers and the song "Only You" by The Platters starts to play on a jukebox I had not noticed until now.

"You came prepared," I compliment him.

"That wasn't even part of the pitch. I just came up with it when I said 'only you'. The jukebox wasn't even there before."

"And you need me to change lives?"

"All these things we can do, we can't do them on earth. We can't even get there. So we wind up with these broken souls trying to fix things here, on the fly, and it's too late."

"Why don't you wipe their bad memories when they arrive?"

"They wouldn't be who they are, so we wouldn't know how to serve them."

"Can they have a mulligan?"

"Those are intended for limited experiences, not bad ones. Exceptions are possible, but it's a high bar."

"And if they don't clear it?"

"Hopefully they find peace and comfort in what we have to offer."

"If not?"

"They can go stardust whenever they want."

"That sounds kind of ruthless."

"I agree. So do my fellow administrators. Part of our job is fielding complaints from the managers, and what the managers complain about most is the misery of so many in their caseload. Which is why we want to work with you. Imagine paving a sunny path for those cloudy spirits before they get here."

I consider ordering that drink, but want to make sure my attention span is fully extended, and even the mild buzz ceiling fermented into afterlife alcohol may hinder that extension.

"How?" I ask.

The administrator leans forward, eager to explain.

"We target three categories: grief, guilt, and trauma. Grief and guilt are layups. Easy fixes. You visit residents who died suddenly, accidentally, under unique circumstances, the kind where they left someone more bereaved than your average mourner. You gather information that proves you met them here, then bring it back to earth to console or exonerate their loved one. You won't have to be anyone other than yourself."

"And by not having to be anyone other than myself," I follow up. "You mean in terms of my personality. How I carry myself, not actually being someone else."

"Trauma is trickier," he leans back, in need of more space to come up with an explanation. "You need to get more than information from the residents. They wronged the people they left behind, so you need confessions, apologies, remorse. This is when posing as a projection comes in handy."

"I can do that?"

"A projection with self-determination," he feeds my curiosity. "Not the nodding toadies designed to flatter the residents and keep the simulation humming. You'll still be you, with your talent for persuasion, your way with words, but you can look and sound like anyone you need to be in order to employ those skills in the most ideal package for the situation."

I grip the edge of the table with both hands.

"I know," he notes my grasp. "It's a lot. But exciting, no?"

"We have a problem."

"Already?"

"Trisha," I drag the name out of my mouth. "The woman I rely on to get me here."

"What about her?"

"She only agreed to send me here again if I agreed to retrieve information for her."

"Great!" he sees a silver lining. "She's on the same page as us."

"No," I wave away the shine he wants to see. "No. It's the back of whatever page you're on. A twisted, hairy, scary back."

"Are you sure?"

"People are going to pay a price for the information I bring her."

"Charging money for something doesn't necessarily make it bad."

"When I say 'price', I don't necessarily mean money."

"Maybe she wants to encourage people to make changes in their lives."

A laugh spurts out of me.

"You're sweet," I manage to suppress the remaining laughter. "Much nicer than I imagined when I saw that fedora. And you're not wrong. I have no doubt she wants to force people to make changes. But only for her benefit. There is no way anything good comes from working with that person. My plan is to go back and tell her I couldn't get what she wanted, that it turns out I really hadn't visited the afterlife before. It was a hallucination, a dream, whichever feels right in the moment when I have to lie to her face."

"Then you won't be able to come back."

The jukebox finishes playing "Only You". The next song is another oldie, but not a hit. One of those songs that faded along with the era, but apparently meant something to the someone whose jukebox we are borrowing.

"Your offer is the best thing I could have imagined," I look around the tiki bar with the customers dressed in formal wear. "If I could ever imagine such a thing. But if she finds out I made it here again, she won't be satisfied with just me. She'll build a clone army to cross over and pile up the intelligence for sale."

"Not a problem," he narrates the visual tour I am taking of the tiki bar. "We patched the clone hole after your last visit."

I stop scanning the room and restore eye contact with him.

"We made an exception for you," he greets my gaze.

I am relieved and flattered.

I fiddle with the offer again.

"I'm the only one that can go through the clone hole," I confirm, so that I can say 'clone hole' again.

Marlowe nods.

"You would give me names whenever I'm 'in town,'" I confirm to actually confirm.

"Unless you can think of a way to market your services on earth," he smirks for a zig before zagging into seriousness. "On that note, we trust you'll use the utmost discretion when giving people their messages, and encourage them to likewise keep it on the down low."

"How many people are you hoping to serve?"

"We'll start small, see how long it takes on average to reach someone and give them the good news, then build from there."

"And tell ourselves the more good missions we can cram in on one side of the ledger, the more it balances out the bad ones Trisha sends me on."

"Limit her to one per trip," he suggests.

"I can tell her how complicated it is to run her errands," I run with the suggestion.

"We won't just balance things out, we'll tip the scales so the good outweighs the bad by a ton."

"You think your boss will see it that way?"

He looks down and taps an offbeat drumroll on the table, providing fanfare to introduce the point he wants to make.

"Think of how big and complex the earth is," he says.

"Okay."

"Are you picturing it?"

"Yes," I am.

"Now think of the number one billion. How large that number really is, not just the word people throw around. How if you count to one million a hundred times you're only one-tenth of the way there."

"Got it."

"Now multiply the size and complexity of earth by five billion."

"Such is your world," I suppose.

"Just our little department."

"Not a lot of interaction with your boss, then."

"We never hear from the regional board. The executive board is practically a myth. Apparently we get a visit from regional when we finally exhaust an era we're responsible for, when the last person from that timeline goes stardust, and we're assigned a new one. Rumor has it the last time that happened is when we transitioned from what you refer to as the Bronze Age to the Industrial Revolution."

"Rumor has it?" I puzzle over the phrase.

"That's the legend."

"I assumed you were all immortal here."

"We are. I guess. Our lives never seem to end."

"So you were there when the last transition happened."

"Probably. But I've had a lot on my plate since then."

"Okay," I nod my way into appreciating the nuances of immortality before returning to a more relatable concept of time. "What about the spaces in between the Bronze Age and the Industrial Revolution? That's quite a jump."

"Other departments were in charge of those, or still are, depending on how quickly people are cycling through. The older eras have fewer people, but they tend to stick around the afterlife longer. They take a while to grow dissatisfied."

"Ah," I claim victory. "That's what my friend Phil and I thought."

"Anyway," he continues, "the departments take over future epochs as they develop and the old ones run out of residents."

"Is there still a department in charge of cave people? I'm asking for Phil, if I ever see him again."

"I wouldn't know. Not my department."

"Any idea how far back your department goes?"

"Beyond the Bronze Age I imagine. Maybe we had cave people at some point."

"But you wouldn't remember."

"Even if time exists, the work we do beats it into oblivion. It takes us thousands of years, from your perspective, to get everyone through an era. The past and the future are too distant to comprehend. We are always in the present."

"Doesn't anyone keep a record?"

"The board."

"That you never hear from."

"The same."

"Then why the sneaking around? The espionage? The trench coat? If you don't think your boss is all-knowing, why not just make me an offer?"

"We may not now if there's a God, or life on other planets. Earth is our territory. Aside from what happens after you die on earth, we don't know any more than you do about the big questions. But I suspect the answer to all of the above is yes. I wouldn't speculate on what any of it looks like or sounds like, but there is a feel to it, and I have a feeling it's best to take precautions."

"You're my contact now," I assume.

"No more manager," he confirms. "No other members of the administration. I consult with them, they're my colleagues, but I'm taking the fall if this doesn't work."

"What shall I call you?"

"Marlowe," he says with a sliver of pride in search of validation.

"As in Philip Marlowe?"

"Oh, it's a last name?"

"He was a private eye in a bunch of books and movies."

"I knew that. Can't you tell?"

"There's the coat and the hat. And the front of the bar, except for the door."

"How about my performance?"

I size up the material and sculpt an answer.

"I think you're more like the mysterious powerful person who hires him."

He brightens.

"Does that mean we have a deal?"

"I'd like to test drive the simulation crasher mode, or whatever you call it."

"Of course," he agrees. "Using it to follow through on Trisha's request might be a good route to take."

I chafe at the suggestion.

"Whether you share it with her is up to you," he addresses my irritation. "But it's your round-trip ticket if you need it."

"Do I give you the person's name?" I concede. "Likely locations?"

"If you have those, that's all you need."

"She gave me a physical description."

"That's more for after you arrive. Keeping it simple keeps us far enough apart so we can both claim plausible deniability."

"What about the shape-shifting trick, the thing with the projections?"

"You have to work with existing projections," he explains. "You can't make up your own. When you reach a simulation and you decide it's best to go incognito, check out the projections to see which one you want to be. Then face them, and clap your hands on the sides of their head, a hand on each ear at the same time, one time, hard."

"Seriously?"

"Like you're playing the cymbals, ready to bang out the last note of a song, and their head is in the way of your cymbals."

"That's ridiculous."

"It's a unique action, which is what our contacts in the Projections Department need to recognize it's you, to know the projection is not being struck as part of the simulation."

"Does the projection, uh, enter me? Do I enter it? What happens next?"

"It envelops you, of course."

"Of course?" I question why this would be obvious.

"Well, if you enveloped the projection, where would that leave your body? An empty husk on the floor?"

"Is that what happens to the projection after I clap its head?"

"They don't have an essence separate from their form. You wear them like a suit."

"And when I'm done with the suit?"

"You're stuck with it until you exit the simulation. It disappears when you leave. So choose your projection carefully."

"That's fine. I was afraid you were going to say I had to clap my own ears. What about your contacts in the Projections Department?"

"What about them?"

"You said you're taking the fall if things go sideways, but they'll be implicated if the board finds out."

"They can easily plead they were just following orders. The running joke about those who work in projections is that it takes one to know one."

Marlowe straying from basic information into comedy strikes me as a good cue to launch myself into a simulation. I lean back, close my eyes, and think of high school football games and aquariums and how much Cam Lamp should go by Cameron.

"Before you go," he interrupts my flow.

"Yes?" I open my eyes and suppress a sigh.

"Could you do us a favor?"

"Do I have a choice?"

"No."

"What is it?"

"Please check in with Devin, too."

"You're joking."

"If you become an afterlife regular, we need to head off any confusion before it happens. Let him know you might be around."

"If I become an afterlife regular, I promise I will do everything in my power to avoid him."

"But one of our clients might get you two mixed up."

"I'll use a fake name. I'll use a new one for each case if I have to."

"That only takes you so far. Your essence is the same as his."

I move to object.

"Physically," he adds. "Your shared essence is purely physical. All right? But because of that, the system may drop him into a simulation instead of you. We need to anticipate that possibility, as remote as it may be."

I exhale long enough to eventually make Marlowe seem more interested in how long it will last rather than what I say afterwards.

"Fine," I finally squeeze in. "I'll check in with Devin."

"Thank you."

I shrug in lieu of a you're-welcome.

"He'll be easy to find," he assures me. "Given the connection you...well, you know. Your physical essence being what it is. The trick is to stay out of sight when you get there. Maybe have a hat and sunglasses in place when you arrive."

"Can I borrow your hat?"

"I think it may stand out rather than blend in."

"Which is why you wore it to our top secret meeting."

"If we get caught, it's going to take a while. I thought I made that clear."

"So you wore it simply because you thought it looked good."

He looks as though he wants to ask "Doesn't it?" but tugs the brim instead and tries to remember what it looks like on his head.

I watch him reconsider his wardrobe and wish I had not teased him. I wonder how high up the hierarchy a person has to climb to find a master of the afterlife who is not insecure about their relationship to earth. I want to ask Marlowe if they have an expression that laments not being able to choose the planet they were assigned, the kind of proverb that circulates around the office when earth is being especially annoying. But given all the languages they speak for the sake of the residents, they may not have a native tongue of their own, no words to build explanations for their feelings, so rather than verbalize an apology disguised as an interest in something about his culture that may not exist, I decide to visit Devin first as a show of good faith.

I start to tell him, but before I can, find myself in what I assume is Devin's current simulation, my abrupt entry most likely due to the strong physical essence we share.

Or so I mutter.

I have no memories of Devin attending a mixed martial arts event, but he appears to have taken an interest in it since dying. I am a few steps up from the ringside seats in a packed arena. I scan the faces to see if I can find him, then think he could be in the ring, playing the role of a fighter, pummeling someone to the delight of a roaring crowd. I turn my attention to the ring and find two unfamiliar figures squaring off. I am disappointed, since I hoped for a moment maybe it could be the other way around, that he would subject himself to a pummeling, the crowd cheering, or better yet booing, as penance for the life he led on earth.

Looking to the ring still leads me to him. He may not be inside of it, but he has a front row seat, which makes more sense.

Jane also has a front row seat, next to him, which makes a lot less sense.

# Chapter Six

A fedora would fit right in. They are everywhere, a variety of shiny updates louder than the classic beige Marlowe sported. I see ads around the arena for casinos and a "Visit Las Vegas" campaign, which makes me wonder if he and Jane also went to the dog show she originated. The thought makes me jealous, but this is Las Vegas with a Devin twist, so her production may not have made the cut.

I walk slowly around the arena from my side to theirs, keeping watch, waiting for one of them to leave the other for a bathroom or beverage break. The current match appears to be part of the undercard lineup, as the arena is half-filled with fans and filled even less with enthusiasm. When the bout ends, a steady stream of bodies files for the doors to the lobby while the fighters stand in the center of the ring awaiting the decision. Devin excuses himself and joins the lobby-bound. I follow him and wait to make sure he is not aiming for the bathroom. When he gets in line for a beer instead, I summon a dark baseball cap with no logo onto my head and a pair of aviator sunglasses to provide plenty of facial coverage.

"Don't freak out," I stand in line next to him.

He looks over and his eyes balloon.

"Holy..." he catches himself. "All right, I'm sorry, I need to freak out a little bit."

"Do it quietly."

"You died already? I thought we designed you better than that."

"I'm on another round trip."

"Oh no," his face drops. "Are you in business with Trisha?"

"What do you mean?"

"How else would you get here without dying?"

"No, I mean why are you so concerned about me getting into business with Trisha? You were in business with her."

"Because she's the only person in the cloning industry who's sleazy enough to go along with what I wanted to do."

"That tracks," I forgive myself for not making that connection before. "I haven't committed. This is a trial run. I'm thinking of pretending nothing happened when I get back."

"Pretend," he advises. "Pretend hard."

"You haven't heard what they're offering me on this end."

"You worked out a deal with the afterlife brass?"

"I was able to crash your simulation without you knowing," I gesture at the surroundings. "You think I could do that without them knowing?"

"And you can do that to anyone?"

"In any form," I nod. "I can become any of the projections in a simulation."

He takes me by the elbow and walks us out of line.

"Afterlife beer won't cut it right now."

He stops us in light traffic away from the main sweep of the crowd.

"Why would they let you do all that?" he asks.

"To help people on earth. Connect with the ex-people over here they miss or thought they wronged and bring back intel letting them know it's all good in the great beyond."

"The afterworld wants to expand," he arrives at his own summary.

"They want to help people before they get here," I defend their goal.

"How did you even come up with this?"

"It wasn't my idea," I confess. "I came here to look for Kelly's dad, not strike a deal."

"Kelly's dad? As in my assistant Kelly?"

"Yup."

"One of people who murdered me?"

"She thought someone murdered her Dad. He went missing for a while, her family thought the worst, and she wanted proof."

"Did you find him here?"

"I did."

"When you tell her, could you also give her a message from me?"

"No."

"Tell her karma's a bitch."

"I will not."

"A bigger one than she is."

"She had the least to do with what happened."

"She didn't do anything to stop it."

"Her dad had nothing to do with it, and he's a good man."

"I wouldn't know."

"You met him before."

"I did?"

"I have a memory of you meeting him."

"Didn't leave a mark."

"Of course not. He wasn't an investor or a networking opportunity."

"You steer every conversation between us into an indictment of my character."

"Where else is there to go?"

He channels his frustration into a new direction.

"How did Kelly even think to ask you about a return trip, anyway?"

The answer seems obvious to me, but I was part of it, and have lived with it longer.

"The shocking information you gave me," I explain. "Those things only you could know that I brought back to throw in their faces and make sure no money was left on the table. Time passed, her Dad disappeared, and she became more curious than scared."

He mulls over his role in giving away our position.

"What happened to him, anyway?"

"He was having an affair with the wife of a big shot businessman, and the big shot caught on and had them killed."

"Both of them?"

"They're great company. Wonderful hosts. Knowing their backstory makes an evening with them painfully beautiful."

"What about when his wife shows up?" he checks if I saw Jane sitting next to him.

"I'm sure they've talked about it," I confirm that I did. "They're smart people. I'd introduce you to them, but I don't think my supervisor would approve."

"I wasn't planning on seeing her," he drops the pretense. "You know that. I made it clear. And it was easy at first. The projections helped. I tried everything with them. In fact, the reason I got interested in mixed martial arts is because I played out an old fantasy of mine that takes place in the middle of an arena like this. It was me and five projections that look like my first prom date, and when we take our robes off..."

"No, no," I hold up a hand. "I get it. Living the afterlife can be tougher than people think. And I'm really glad the only memories we share are from earth."

"I wasn't interested in forming human connections," he proceeds. "I tried with my grandma and grandpa, but I can't bear to be in the same simulation with either of them. All they do is complain about each other."

"Is your grandpa still with Angela?"

He rolls his eyes.

"Have you checked in with Aunt Gladys?" I ask.

"A bit much," he winces. "I don't know what happened between you two, but she's even more intense than she was before. I can't keep up. All she wants to do is ask me questions and give me advice, like she's a life coach or something. Phil, on the other hand..."

"Isn't Phil the best?"

We bond over Phil.

"Thank you," he puts a hand on my shoulder. "Everyone should have a friend like Phil."

"The world would be a better place. Both worlds would be better places."

"The more I hung out with Phil, the more I thought maybe I could be a decent enough person to look up Jane."

I still would prefer not to think of them being together.

"I met her husband," I say to both inform and obstruct.

"Oh yeah?" he seems interested rather than put off. "She never talks about him."

"Turned out to be a nice enough guy, considering how much he didn't want to see you."

"Where did you meet him?"

"I went to his apartment."

"You did?"

"I thought one of their daughters would benefit from a tutoring program I funded."

"Her oldest."

"Yes."

"She talks about the girls a lot."

"And you don't mind?"

"No," he takes offense. "So has her daughter benefitted from the tutoring program I funded?"

"She has, from what I hear."

"I figured you'd get into charity work."

"Your money is doing a lot of good."

"I'll bet no one knows it's my money."

"Always anonymous," I confirm.

"Naturally," he grins.

I look around, so surprised at how well we are getting along that I wonder if maybe there is an afterworld representative manipulating events.

"Jane won't come looking for me," he assumes something else about my scan of the crowd. "We're doing okay, but I think she appreciates plenty of lengthy breaks."

I consider correcting him, but would not know what to say.

"I wish there was a way I could thank you," he says. "Besides just saying 'thank you'. Some way I could pay you back."

"No need," I assure him. "I'm glad to see those relationships flourishing."

"And surprised?"

"So much so I almost forgot to let you know why I paid you a visit."

"It wasn't to spy on me?"

"I'm supposed to let you know, since I may be commuting to the afterworld if I take the job, there's a chance the mechanism may drop you into a simulation instead of me thanks to our special connection."

"Ooh. Do I get to complete the mission if that happens?"

"I think they'll fix it pretty quickly."

"Who are they?"

"I'm working with administration."

"The next rung up."

"Yup."

"You get to meet the big cheese?"

"There's about a million more rungs before that happens. This operation makes the largest company on earth look like a churro cart."

"So they're paying you under table?" he suspects.

"If they were paying me, yes."

"Oh my goodness," he beams. "I love the afterlife. At this rate I'm never going stardust."

"It would make my job a lot easier if you did."

"Hey," he ignores my jab to make way for an idea. "What does Trisha want you to do while you're here?"

"Get information about someone she used to know. Proof of afterlife."

"That's it? Nothing shady yet?"

"As far as I can tell."

"Do you have space in your schedule for anything else?"

"I'm in storage for two weeks, however that translates."

"I've got an idea for a real trial run," he says. "Something that will give you a long look at whether you want to work for her."

"I'm listening."

"Get revenge on the man who killed Kelly's father."

"What?"

"That's the way this gig is going to play out, right? You run a blackmail scheme for Trisha, and humanitarian aid for some administrative bleeding hearts."

"Pretty much."

"Pretty much," he accuses me of being naive. "The good Samaritan stuff sounds great, especially since you get to jump around from sim to sim and morph into any projection you want. But have you really thought about where those errands for Trisha are going to lead?"

"I've tried not to."

"Well here's your chance," he leads us farther away from the path of the projections passing by.

"What," I note the stealthy maneuver, "the projections are going to eavesdrop on us?"

"Habit," he explains. "An involuntary action based on a lifetime of shady dealing."

"Why don't I remember more of that shady dealing?"

"You know why."

"Because you don't have a conscience."

"I'd prefer you say *didn't* have one, but go ahead. Judge me. This is where my past becomes an asset. Check back in with Kelly's father and his lover. Get some information from her. Really personal stuff. Intimate, haunting details about her and her husband. Things that will make the guy jump out a window."

"He's a big deal," I hedge. "I don't know how I could deliver any of it."

"I've got a guy in the valley who can set you up with the kind of account you need. It's untraceable, buried deep on the web, like in the Mariana Trench of the web. Even if you don't use it on the killer cuck, you want an account like this if you take the job with Trisha. Don't ever let her send you to meet someone in person."

"Good thinking."

"The account guy is weird, as you can probably imagine. Maybe the weirdest man I've ever met in my life, but that's a high bar in the valley, so I'll let you be your own judge."

He turns to the stream of fight fans milling past.

"Anyone have a pen and paper?" he asks them.

A woman in an airbrushed t-shirt that says "Queen Bee" stops and pulls what Devin needs from the back pocket of her denim shorts.

"Thank you," he tells her before turning to me and saying he thought it was going to be the guy with the fake UFC title belt cinched around his sweat pants.

"I can never quite corral the projections in my simulations, either," I sympathize.

"You'll find our boy in one of these three McDonalds," he jots them down as he speaks. "Got any of my memories of him?"

"The valley is full of dudes spread out with their laptops at fast food restaurants."

"He'll recognize you."

"So do a lot of geeks in the area. It's one of the reasons I moved."

"This is different. You'll see. More of an acknowledgement. No gaping."

He hands me the completed list.

"Oh good," I look it over. "I already know where these are. I don't think a piece of paper can make the jump back."

"He's going to want a very specific form of payment. No cash, always something different. Once he asked me for a round-trip ticket to Phuket, another time it was a commemorative plate."

"Commemorating what?"

"Alaskan statehood."

"Ah," a vision stirs. "I remember. You found it at an antique mall."

"I did."

"Where was that place? How did you know where to look?"

"He provides explicit directions on how to get what he wants. It's not a scavenger hunt. That's no way to build a customer base."

"Might be fun, though."

"If one has the time."

"There's never enough time on earth."

"Here, though…" he trails off.

"Nothing but time here," I complete his thought.

We seem to agree that our conversation has run its course.

"I should get back to my seat," he says.

"Yes," I follow through on the exit strategy he has provided. "I wasn't actually looking for her earlier, but I am now."

"Thanks for letting me know I might suddenly find myself in a strange simulation."

"Thanks for the advice and the connection."

"Connections are what we're all about."

"Maybe I'll look you up if I take the job. Bounce some ideas off you."

"Dark, morally-dubious ideas?"

"No," I protest but realize I was thinking that very thing.

"It's okay," he extends a hand. "Our roles are well-established. And I established them."

"I couldn't ask for worse parents than you and Trisha," I accept his offer. "But it's led to an interesting ride."

He pats my shoulder with his other hand while releasing his grip.

"Be the best version of a better me you can be," he says.

I watch him blend into the crowd filing back for the main event as I piece together the expression he just made up. I revel in our pleasant parting for a moment before it starts to feel misplaced. Not that I find anything wrong with getting along, but we seem like a pair who fit best when we entertain each other close to the edge of love and hate, or at least the edge of tolerance and irritation.

With this in mind, I notice a projection in the form of a stylishly bedraggled young man designed to be the centerpiece of a rowdy party, and ask him if he would please help me find my pet ferret that jumped off my shoulder and scurried into a nearby supply room.

"No way!" he spouts.

"Why not?" I ask.

"No," he laughs. "I'll help you, bro. But I mean, a ferret? No way!"

"Ah, okay," I lead us down the corridor. "Thank you."

It dawns on me that since this is not my simulation, I cannot make the room appear where I want it to be, so we walk longer than I anticipated to find one.

"Where is this room, bro?" he asks.

"Never mind," I stop and look around to see if anyone is watching. "Can I tell you something?"

"Sure."

I turn to face him.

"This might sound weird."

I line him up in front of me.

"What?" he asks.

I clap his ears, as Marlowe instructed, like clashing a pair of cymbals together.

I disappear. The place where I was standing is empty. I am seeing it from his perspective, which is now mine.

I feel no different, as if where he stood is the only thing I took. I look down at my body and discover I have in fact taken much more.

I am him.

I touch my face to make sure it completes the package, but it feels like mine.

I find my reflection in a glass frame covering an advertisement for an upcoming performance, and see that I do look like him, like it. Like Marlowe said, it is indeed a costume that I am now wearing, a costume that does not touch my body, but surrounds it.

I set out for where Devin and Jane are seated. I spend my first several steps wondering what is underneath all the human facades that pass by, now that I have one of my own. I wait for the other projections to compliment me on my cloak, to be recognized as one of them, and collect inside information they only share among themselves. By the time I am back inside the seating area, I sack the idea of a secret projection society. We are nothing but borrowed faces flowing through a simulation.

The fighters have not made their entrance yet, which allows me to make mine.

"Devin!" I call out with ten yards remaining before I reach their seats. "Yo! Devin!"

My voice is also that of the foppish party hopper.

Devin and Jane both turn around and track my course with confusion. Jane is in the aisle seat, so all business must be conducted over and around her.

"What's up, my man?" I reach past Jane for an arm-wrestle style shake from Devin.

"Do I know you?" he remains seated and refuses to engage.

"Aw, come on, dude," I pull back my hand and run it through my hair. "You don't remember?"

"No," he insists more to Jane than to me.

"That time in this arena, with the five twins, or whatever you call five chicks that look alike."

"Hmm," Jane makes a show of putting her hand to her chin in artificial contemplation. "What *do* you call five chicks that look alike? Is it the same term for five dudes that look alike? Or do chicks have their own word?"

"Uh..." Devin panics at the thought of the simulation getting away from him and taking on a mind of its own. He looks around for any other signs that he is losing control, and in doing so, scans his way to a realization.

He turns his attention back to me and his fear dissolves into a big grin.

"Sir?" I hear a voice behind me.

I turn to find a security guard waiting to escort me away.

"Aw, Devin," I play along. "Not cool, man."

He shrugs and would probably wink at me, but doing so might give up the game, even though Jane still has her glare fixed in my direction.

As the security guard scoots me up the stairs, Jane turns her glare onto Devin, which gives me a chance to follow through on a wink between us. He tries to keep a straight face as she tries not to berate him in front of their section.

We reach the main track that circles the venue and I let the guard know with a wave I intend to use it. As I walk I wonder whether my next stop should be my follow-up with the star-crossed lovers to plot their revenge, or my introduction to Cam Lamp to stamp my passport for Trisha.

Since all deals are off if I fail to bring back dirt on the Lamp incident, I decide to check in with him. Plus the first fighter has emerged to swagger his way to the ring, which brings the arena to their feet with a roar, which reminds me to think of a high school football game as a landing spot.

The roar remains, but its volume lowers and its intensity relaxes. The crowd shrinks, and I am walking a straight line in the front row of a rectangle of bleachers, outdoors on a cool evening. As the crowd settles down after the play that excited them, I ask the projection in the front row if I can have his jacket. He takes it off and hands it over.

I put it on and complete my walk to the end of the row, the lowest and farthest point in the bleachers, so I can survey the crowd for a man who looks like he is peering through a pair of binoculars.

My initial probe of a hundred faces comes up empty, and I turn my attention to the field to give my eyes a timeout.

The players stand and fidget along the sideline. Most of them watch the game, some joke with one another, and one at the very end is involved in a conference with an older man who wears relaxed-fit pants and a golf pullover. I assume he is a coach. He wraps up what he has to say, pats the kid on the shoulder pad, and walks toward the stands, proving my assumption wrong. He is not a coach.

As he draws closer to the stairs leading up to the bleachers, I notice he has a particular squint, his upper lip straining above his teeth while his lower lip remains relaxed. I turn to the nearest projection, a woman who looks like she has logged a lot of miles in a minivan.

"Who is that guy?" I ask her.

"The kid's father," she replies.

"What's his name?"

"The father or the kid?"

"The father."

"Mr. Lamp."

"Cameron?"

"Cam," she nods.

I watch him walk up the stairs into the stands.

"Very dedicated," I comment.

"Very," she confirms.

The elder Lamp finds a seat but does not hold still. One leg jiggles a couple of shakes per second while he repeatedly locks, unlocks, then relocks his fingers together as if finding the perfect prayer formation.

"I don't imagine he likes anyone talking to him during the game," I say.

"He doesn't like anyone talking to him at all."

"Oh yeah?"

"It's his simulation," she recites the rule. "We're just here to cheer on his kid."

I am surprised to find self-awareness in a projection. I want to ask how much she knows about her existence, what more she wants to know, and if all projections are like her, but fear even one question may unravel more than this one simulation. I have been granted so much freedom, and would not want to come across as ungrateful.

"Okay then," I take a seat and look out at the field. "I'll wait until halftime to talk to him."

I assume she is staring at me in disbelief. I glance over to check, and unlike my assumption about Cam being a coach, this time I am correct.

# Chapter Seven

His son plays defensive back, but the other team runs the ball almost every down, attempting only a couple of wobbly passes, so he sees little action other than arriving late to the pile when a run is called in his direction. Watching Cam watch the game is more interesting than watching the game. I size up a few projections in the stands that might be worth wearing, but decide to stick with myself. The weary consciousness of the minivan mom has me reluctant to clap any more ears until I can talk to Marlowe about how much the projections know. Cam never met Devin, as far as my memories are concerned, and does not seem like a heavy gamer or tech buff, but in case my usual name triggers a random recognition, I think of a name to use, what I think of as a "fake name" at first, but in a moment recognize it as no more fake than the name I have been using or the name I have been called.

As I watch the game clock on the scoreboard tick away the minutes until halftime, most of what I design involves how to approach the upcoming situation. Unlike the program Marlowe and the administration wants to set up, I am not obligated to deliver any messages to the son when I return to earth. Likewise, I suspect what Trisha wants now differs from what she will want in the future. I am here to satisfy her curiosity rather than her ambition.

When the horn signals the end of the first half, the team jogs toward the edge of the bleachers where I am seated, heading for the building behind us.

Cam takes a brisk walk along the front row to intercept the line as they run past. He crosses in front of me and flags down his son, who veers away from the herd to hear what his father has to say.

"You know what to do," Cam leans over the railing for emphasis. "That's all you can do."

His son nods and rejoins the stampede.

Cam stands up straight and watches them go with a wistful squint as they disappear around the corner.

"Projections don't have freewill," I say for his benefit. "We try to give it to them, but they always end up doing what we want them to do."

He levels his squint at me, the wistfulness smothered by a battle between confusion and anger.

"What did you say?" he seems afraid to ask.

"That is a projection, right?" I ask for verification, even though I know the answer. "Not your actual son."

"Is this a malfunction?" he looks around in search of a manager.

"This is a new program sponsored by the powers that be, designed to help residents work through residual earth trauma."

"What makes them think I have residual earth trauma?"

"Maybe you don't," I stand up. "Maybe they're casting too wide a net to look for candidates to pilot this program. But they're finally acknowledging that letting people loose in the afterlife without addressing their previous life does not serve anyone's interests, and I commend them for that."

"Are you one of them, like the guy, or whatever he was, who checked me in, or something else?"

"I'm Trey," I extend my hand. "I can tell you that much."

"Cam," he shakes it.

"A pleasure to meet you, Cam," I conclude our handshake. "Not to dodge your question. I mean, I'd certainly like to think of myself as something else, in the most flattering definition of the term, but you know how it is here. What we are, or who we are, isn't the point. How we can serve you is the point. Shall we?"

I gesture for us to take a walk together toward the stairs. He accepts as if hypnotized, walking in a mental fog heavy enough to lead him off a ledge if we were heading toward one. I make sure to beat him to the stairs so I can escort him down. As I guide the way, I lock eyes with the minivan mom for an instant. She appears interested in joining us. I look at the other projections around her and none share her interest. The rules never occur to the others, much less breaking any. When we reach the field, I point us farther away from where we met to keep my back to her.

"If you'll bear with me, Cam, I'd like to ask you some questions that help me help you work through whatever administration thinks might be going on here."

"Sure," he surrenders.

"Thank you, sir. I know this isn't what you were expecting when you fired up this simulation, but we're in this together, for the long haul, and we want to help you lighten the load you're carrying through it all."

"Okay," he lets me guide him along the sideline as though we are strolling through the gardens of an assisted living home.

"So is this about how old your son was when you joined us here?"

"No, he was older. About thirty."

"Do you often revisit this period of your relationship?"

"Yes."

"More than others?"

"Yes."

"To a large degree?"

"Yes."

"What would you say is your second favorite age to visit?"

"When he was even younger, like six or seven years old. He loved going to the aquarium."

"Do you ever simulate phases from his adulthood?"

He stops and stares at the next flight of stairs ahead of us. The marching band walks down them in a line toward the center of the field for their halftime performance.

"Cam?" I try to interrupt his trance.

He walks toward the band. I keep pace.

"Were you on speaking terms?" I ask.

A voice over the public address system announces the entrance of the band.

"He wasn't on the football team," Cam says as though confessing to the tuba player walking past.

"No?"

"He was in the band. He played clarinet."

"That's fine," I assure him. "Most of our residents engage in fantasies rather than re-creations."

"Even when it comes to their kids?"

"When it comes to everything and everyone. You said going to the aquarium is something he really liked to do."

"Yes."

"So it's just this one sim where you play make believe."

"But I do it a lot."

"Why do you think that is?"

He looks across the field at the band as they adopt their opening formation.

"This is when the split started," he says.

"Did you seem him at all after he became an adult?"

"For a while," he stays focused on the band. "There wasn't one big scene where he walked out and slammed the door. It was gradual. Fewer phone calls, fewer lunches. Then he moved. I guess that was kind of a door slam. I didn't think of it that way at the time. It seemed to free him of any obligation he may have still felt to keep in touch. Reaching out became more and more uncomfortable. Eventually I stopped trying."

"What was it about being in the band instead of the football team that started it?"

He tears his attention away from the band and faces me.

"It sounds so stupid, I know. It's not like he was on drugs or hanging out with the wrong crowd. He was a good kid. Just not the kid I expected. I learned a lot playing sports. It made things easy for my father to talk to me. The action of the game takes care of the lessons. All you have to do is comment on what happens."

"You can't do that with band?"

"It's all set. As long as you practice the music and the routine, there are no surprises. All that left me with is reminding him to practice, which of course got tiresome."

The band starts playing their version of a pop song I cannot place.

"A lot of other things happen in life," I raise my voice to speak over the music in the distance. "The unexpected isn't confined to sports."

"But it's contained to a field or a court. That's what makes it easy to comment on. The clichés write themselves. Real-life personal failure is so much harder. Friends, relationships, they're so messy. Even when a sports slogan does apply to real life, it sounds so shallow."

"You can think of a different way to say it."

His lower lip springs into action, turning his squint into the first smile he has flashed since I spotted him.

"That's what I'm doing here," he explains. "Sometimes he's the star, sometimes he never gets in the game. I get to practice new slogans for all occasions, highs and lows, even the long spaces in between where nothing seems to happen, but they still matter."

"You're preparing for when he arrives," I commend him.

"I started when I was still on earth. I went to games and watched the fathers and sons, whether they were on the team or in the band, looking for tips on how to repair what I had broken, or more like what I had neglected. I was visiting a past that never existed. I tried the aquarium too every once in a while, but there wasn't much to learn. The kids are so young at that point. It's about keeping an eye on them, feeding them, and refusing to buy them souvenirs. My son and I were okay back then, anyway. The aquarium was more about reminiscing."

He listens to the band. I join him and we take in the rest of the song. I finally recognize it as "Ms. Jackson" by Outkast, a song about convincing ourselves we are worthy of the person we are with. At least that is how Devin thinks of it. I wonder if the melody stuck with him out of affection or spite for the people who did not stick with him.

"If you don't mind my asking," I wait until the break between songs. "What brought you here before you had a chance to reconnect with him?"

"You don't know?"

"Not my department," I rely on the line every afterlife bureaucrat leans on.

"My second wife, the woman I married after divorcing my son's mother," he loses himself in the recollection. "That was a whole other source of contention between him and me."

"What about your second wife?" I pull him back into our exchange.

"Oh," he replants himself. "Sorry."

"That's fine."

"She murdered me."

The band breaks into the first note of the next song.

"What?" I screech above the blare of the second note.

"She choked me," he breaks the news as if it is the weather report on a mild day.

"With her bare hands?"

"It was a piece of cake."

"I can't imagine strangling someone is easy."

"No," he clarifies. "It was an actual piece of cake."

"Ah," I remember. "That's right."

"I thought you said you didn't know."

"Well," I scramble for cover. "I mean, sometimes I jump ahead, trying to guess the next move, and I have to remind myself to hold back and let the patient do the talking."

"The patient?"

"The client," I want to get back to where we were. "Whatever you prefer. I'm really curious to know how a piece of cake can be used as a murder weapon."

He looks me over before continuing.

"It helps to use a certain kind of cake," he says.

"Very thick and rich," I presume.

"She went with a flourless chocolate torte."

"That seems like a good choice."

"It worked for her."

"How exactly did she make it work?"

The cause of his death stirs a chuckle out of him, but moving into the memory sobers him up.

"We were on a cruise," he recalls. "All you can eat buffets, but no food allowed in the rooms. We decided to break the rules one night, be bad. Or she did, and it sounded fun to me. We were like that. You know, reverting to a kind of juvenile relationship after going through the serious business of our marriages dissolving. Dessert made the most sense. Appetizers and side dishes aren't sexy, and you can't really sneak out a main course. Even if you could..."

"Not sexy," I feed into his philosophy.

He appreciates my understanding.

"She wrapped a couple slices of torte and two forks in a napkin," he proceeds. "Then she carefully hid the package in her clutch. She had a different matching clutch for each of her outfits she laid out for the cruise. We barely managed to keep it together as we left the dining room, giggling all the way. I'll spare you the details of what happened when we got back to our room, up until the moment in question. Eventually she crawled on top of me with her knees on my hands, pinning my arms down by my side."

"Harder to lift your arms than to lower them," I pitch in.

"If she had pinned me by the elbows above my head, which is what most people would probably do, it seems to be the standard submissive position, I would have been able to break free. But keeping my arms down like that, I should have known something was off."

"Hindsight."

"That's what I tell myself. Being fed chocolate torte by the woman I loved was pretty distracting."

I find it interesting that he mentions his love for her right as we reach the part where she kills him. A reflexive grunt gives away my position.

He spots me.

I have no choice but to come out of my hiding place.

"You must have really loved her," I explain.

"I never noticed she was killing me until it was too late."

"Love," I summarize.

We watch the band perform for a measure. I look back into the stands to see if I can spot the mindful projection, but the only faces I find are ambivalent, playing their part.

"Our last seconds together were made of long, slow kisses," Cam brings his story to a head. "A kiss before feeding me an extremely large bite, and another kiss to make sure it stayed lodged in my throat."

I wonder how much Trisha knows, how much her mother told her. The information I examined to prepare for my trip was limited. No references to cake, much less what kind, or that he was in his room, and his wife was with him. When I deliver what I learned, I can stop short of revealing that her mother gave him the kiss of death. There are plenty of details up until that point, enough evidence to prove I met the man.

I can go now. I have what I need. He is back to watching the band, losing himself in their music and his memories. Maybe it would be for the best if I was not there when he turned my way, or if he addressed me while still staring at the field and was met with silence. But if feels wrong. The earth stumped him enough. No need for the afterlife to contribute.

"Thank you for participating in the beta test of our new afterlife wellness program," I announce. "I hope you found it helpful."

"So that's it?" he keeps his attention toward the field.

"We encourage members of our beta squad to schedule follow-up appointments with a therapist of their projection, which I know sounds counterproductive, but consider what a therapist does. They mostly listen, and projections are great listeners. Of course you may not feel the need for a follow-up if you think our session was sufficient."

"Is there a survey I can fill out?"

"We don't rely on self-reported data to gauge the opinions of our residents. We go right to the source."

"Reading our minds."

"Mind reading gets confusing pretty quickly. We use it to set up the simulations, but reading much beyond that requires way more energy than is worthwhile. Too many thoughts buzzing around and bumping into each other. We can learn all we need to know by observing your simulations."

"It might be interesting to ask us anyway," he almost looks at me, but does not make a full turn. "See if there's a difference between what people say and what people think."

"Discrepancies are a given. The only question is how wide the gap is between them."

"The session was helpful," he raises his volume to compete with the crescendo that the band is reaching.

"Glad to hear it."

"I might be lying."

"The truth will be revealed."

Halfway through my statement the band stops playing, hurling my words through the night air, where they sail unobstructed over the silence. I wait an uncomfortable couple of seconds for a reaction from Cam, or anyone within earshot, before being saved by a roar from the crowd. The team is jogging back to the sideline in anticipation of the second half. Cam scans the flock for his son, drawn to them on impulse like a border collie. As far as he is concerned, I have already disappeared.

I oblige him by imagining the field is the ocean, the roar of the crowd is the sound of the surf, and I am standing on the bluff where the Arias compound looms. Whether the ground rises beneath me, or the ground in front of me falls and fills with water is hard to gauge. Both may be the case. The sea level teeters and the elevation totters as daylight replaces the night. When it all comes to rest, I feel as if I am on an elevator that has reached its floor. Even though there are no walls and no door, I wait until we seem to have come to a complete stop before turning toward the house.

Kelly's father and Fiona are on their side porch waving me over.

"Perfect timing," I remark as I reach the steps. "Tell me you're not projections keeping an eye on the house while the two real versions of you are off skiing down Everest with snow leopards."

"We didn't think we'd see you again," Fiona says as they both stand and greet me with hugs and pecks on the cheek.

"Does it matter that much to you?" I ask.

"Kind of," she confesses.

"Which kind of surprised us," Arias adds.

"You're not as adventurous as I thought," I tease.

"We don't get out much," she acknowledges.

"We have everything we need here," he gives her a kiss.

"All things freaky and fantastic stay on site," she indulges his kiss.

"Like lemur cabana boys and pelican co-pilots," I try to keep the conversation asexual.

"Those things, too," he tries to keep the conversation suggestive.

"Mind if I sit down?" I take a more physical approach.

"Of course," he backs off and we all take our seats.

"Spectacular day," I note as we settle in.

"Thank you for pointing that out," she says. "We can take it for granted."

"Saying it's a spectacular day is like saying the sky is blue," he says.

"I figured I'd praise the ordinary before I run something by you that's a bit more out of the ordinary."

They share an excited silence.

"Well," he keeps his eyes on her. "Let's strap in then."

I pause as if there really are safety belts they need a moment to buckle. When they peel their attention off each other and toward me, I deliver the news.

"How would you like to exact revenge on the man who killed you?"

They look at one other again, but without sharing their silence. They each have their own.

"A friend of mine in the tech industry built a clone of himself," I edit the details of my story. "Turns out when they put him in storage for future use, it simulates death so closely that he can visit here, like he's on an afterlife tourist visa. He checked in with me during his latest trip and asked if I had any errands that need running."

"My husband is psychotic," Fiona says. "I wouldn't want something so valuable to go anywhere near him. Thank you, but no. I couldn't live with that responsibility."

"You're already past living with responsibility," I add a dash of levity to my appeal.

"You know what I mean," she respects the effort, but not enough to take the deal.

"The clone won't pursue him directly," I make my next move. "Or confront him. I have a heavily encrypted account the clone can use. You tell me some information only you and your husband could possibly know, intimate details, then we use that account to haunt him with those details and drive him insane. We word the messages to look like they're coming from you, a very articulate ghost."

"Why can't she just talk to this clone guy?" Arias asks. "Why does she have to go through you?"

"This isn't something the administration wants to spread around the afterworld. I'm lucky they're letting me take advantage of this connection. It's a pilot program of sorts. What I'm offering is an exclusive opportunity."

"To haunt people and drive them insane?" he retorts. "Why can't I send a message to my daughters and tell them how much I love them and miss them?"

"I can do that, too."

"If we play ball?"

"No, I would do it anyway."

"I don't care," Fiona breaks through. "Incentives or not, I'm in."

She glares at him. He backs off. She continues.

"How do we check to see if it's working?" she asks.

"When you get the message that he's here."

"There's no hell?"

"They've assured me they're working on it."

"Wait a second," Arias re-enters the conversation. "The goal is to kill him?"

"If we drive him crazy enough."

"You got a problem with that?" Fiona glares at him even harder.

"Probably not," he considers the question in earnest. "But I might have a problem listening to you rattle off intimate details about your marriage to someone we barely know."

"So it's fine when I tell you intimate details about my marriage."

"Let's not..." he tries to stop her.

"It turns him on," she informs me.

"We don't..." I take his side.

"Nothing to be ashamed of," she presses on. "Who wouldn't be interested in the sex life of the person who ordered a hit on you?"

"She changes the names," he defends himself to me.

"But he knows who everyone is," she undermines his defense.

"Tell you what," I come upon a compromise. "I don't need complete narratives. All I need are specific details. No blow-by-blow accounts of what happened in a particular situation, just its most prominent features. Key words to let him know there's nowhere to hide."

"Like little plastic dinosaurs in the butt," she offers.

"Yes," I manage my reaction. "Like that."

"Your butt or his?" Arias asks.

"It doesn't matter for what we're trying to do," I encourage them to move on.

"I haven't heard that one before," he insists.

"He would put them in the tapioca pudding on the small of my back," she mixes in a familiar reference.

"Ah," he can see it now.

"Then there were the little dildos shaped like toes," she proceeds.

"No," I shake my head. "Someone could look up your purchase records or his records and find those."

"They were custom made" she explains. "They took molds of my feet."

"All the more reason," I hold the line. "He might think the mold makers are in on it."

"The more options, the better," Arias preaches.

"I suppose."

"Oh!" she remembers another. "The chaise lounge with the hole in it!"

"The one by the pool?" Arias confirms.

"Yes," she grins.

"Perfect," I encourage her.

"Are you going to write these down?" Arias asks me.

"Oh," I check to see if I still have the paper Devin gave me with the McDonalds locations on it.

"Here," he claps his hands and Rennie the red ruffed lemur swings along the trellis with a pen clutched in the toes of his right foot, and a small pad of paper in his left. He flings them at me as he reaches the slat in the trellis closest to where we sit, then swings back in the direction he came from.

I catch the pad of paper but not the pen, and scramble to pick it up.

"All right," I mutter as I open the pad, click the pen, and compose the list. "Little plastic dinosaurs, tapioca, butt, toe dildos, hole in chaise lounge by pool…"

"Speaking of the pool," Arias adds. "What about the thing with the drain?"

"Was there a problem with the drain?" she cannot recall.

"Almost," he drips. "The suction? In the deep end?"

The memory surfaces and she bursts out laughing.

"Maybe," I stop writing, "I should let you two make your list, then you can give it to me when you're done."

I offer the paper and pen.

"Good idea," he snatches them from me.

"I'll give you some space," I stand and walk down the steps toward the bluff.

They form their huddle and begin to brainstorm.

"Oh, and write down his contact info, too, so I know where to send it."

Fiona nods for a second without looking at me, while Arias gives me a wave.

"Phone and email," I add, simply to see if they look my way at all, which they do not.

I am relieved to not hear any more allusions to events that inspire their oral erotic fiction, but realize I will have to memorize the list since the pad will not make it back to the living. I could write the items on my body with a Sharpie. The possibility has me laughing by the time I reach the overhang above the ocean, though I know this body will not make it back either.

I wonder how much time has passed on earth. Two hours? Two days? A week? A company of pelicans flies past. Thanks to the direction our meeting has taken, I am left to not only contemplate if they are the same birds who fly with Fiona, but if they play a role in any erogenous fantasies. I offer a quiet apology to the pelicans and keep walking.

Before long I hear the lovers calling me back, their voices just audible above the surf. I turn to make sure the sound of my name is not my imagination, and see them beckon. I walk back to their palace and they greet me with smiles at the top step.

"Enjoy," Arias presents me with the notepad.

"I'll just hand it over to the clone," I take it from him.

"Aw," Fiona exaggerates a pout. "Really?"

"The list won't mean anything to me, anyway," I gesture with the pad in hand as if tossing it aside. "Just a series of random items."

"You need to use your imagination," she says.

They look at each other in confidence, with confidence.

"No need," I keep my distance. "As long as it does the trick."

I put the notepad in my back pocket as a pretext for my exit.

"We need to stop beating around the bush," Arias squeezes her around the waist.

"You're right," she chuckles and kisses him before facing me. "Would you like to join us in a three-way?"

For all of its magic, the afterlife can be very predictable.

"We were hoping you would join us last time," he pitches in. "But I guess you thought we wanted privacy instead of company."

"Such a gentleman," she adds. "It's part of your appeal."

"Thank you," I say. "And sorry if I misread the room last time."

"You don't seem keen on the idea," he regrets to acknowledge.

"That's a fair assessment."

"I thought for sure someone with your power and money on earth would be down for some fun."

"Not this kind."

"So you agree that it's fun?" he looks for an opening.

"Can't you fill that role with a projection?"

"Of course," she says. "And we have. Often. But we want a real person."

A real person.

If they called me that right away, I may have embraced their offer, and we would already be in their living room, bedroom, pool, or wherever, doing whatever they had in mind.

A real person.

Maybe that lie would wrap itself around me and whisper in my ear more persuasively than either lover, and I would panic and flee. A projection would never back out, only a real person. My escape would make the lie even more believable.

"So it's a no?"

The voice pulls me out of my fantasy about being a real person in their fantasy. I am not sure whose voice it is. They are both smiling, holding out hope, or being polite.

"I'm afraid so."

They console each other with wilting glances.

"It means a lot to me that you asked," I try to cheer them up. "More than you'll ever know."

Arias hooks his arm around her shoulder and clutches it. She reciprocates by kissing him, as though one of them ran for a city council seat and the race has been called for the other candidate early on election night.

"What's the message you'd like to send your daughters?" I ask Arias.

"Excuse me?" he drops out of consoling Fiona.

"The message for your daughters."

"We get it," he gripes. "You're not into a threesome. No need to get self-righteous."

"No," I start over. "You said earlier you were interested in sending them a message, when we were talking about how the clone works."

"Oh," he remembers. "Yes. Sorry. Well…"

He turns his attention back to Fiona.

"Tell them the truth," he proclaims more to her than to me.

She is a captivated audience.

"That I died for the love of my life," he rides the momentum. "And that I love both of them more than life."

All designs on a three-way vanish. They are enough for each other.

I backpedal toward the steps, trying not to disturb them. When I turn around to complete my escape, my shoes scuffle the pavers for a moment.

"Last chance," Fiona half jokes.

I stop in my tracks.

Since honesty turns them on, and they want to close the proceedings with a few more words, I try to extract a little more truth.

"I'm curious," I face them again. "If this works, and your husband winds up here sooner rather than later, are you going to request an appointment with him?"

Their cuddle interrupted, Arias looks at Fiona, who sinks into the question.

"I don't know," she muses. "I think I have to wait and see what it feels like to find out he's here."

"I'll do my best to make sure you get that feeling," I tap the notepad in my back pocket, our weapon of choice, and leave them on the patio like a couple of homesteaders out on the prairie watching the hired gun ride off into the distance.

"Until next time!" Fiona calls after me.

"We promise it won't be weird!" Arias adds.

I raise my arm without quite reaching a wave, and without looking back.

The notepad rubs my behind and reminds me I need to memorize its contents. I have yet to simply sit and enjoy a paradise of my own creation since arriving in this sequel. The ocean reminds me of my open air bar in what I remember of Maui. I start to initiate a jump from this simulation into mine, but my thoughts are pinned by the feeling that a short trip to get there would add a splash of satisfaction. Another ride on a jet ski, or maybe a banana boat, with a marine life escort is tempting, but I would rather not risk smearing the ink. I could rig it so the words would not run, but am feeling more contemplative than adventurous. With no airport in sight, I wonder if a helicopter could make it to the island from here. The sound of rotor blades chopping through the air answers my question. I turn to watch it approach and land a safe distance from me on the bluff. The pilot waves me over and I trot in a crouch toward the back door, which slides open thanks to the efforts of two women in hula dresses who offer a lei greeting and complimentary drink as I sit down.

I thank them and look out the window as we lift off. Kelly's father and Fiona are joined by the rest of their community in front of the compound, the parents and grandparents who look younger than their children and grandchildren. We make a pass over them before heading out to sea. They wave at us, their clothing flapping in the wind generated by the helicopter. I imagine them being blown over, sent tumbling into somersaults, looking as foolish as they insist on behaving, but that kind of mind control only applies to projections. This place is for human consumption, and being manipulated by other humans is no human's idea of heaven.

# Chapter Eight

I sit at a table facing the ocean with my back to the bar. I need to focus on the list and the contact information. When I take a break, I consider my thoughts on manipulation. Even if someone enjoys being manipulated, here in their Eden they are still in charge of making it happen. If I joined in a threesome with Arias and Fiona, and one of them wanted me to boss them around, that would be their choice. They are pushing the button that makes another person push their buttons.

I make sure the ocean is churning with whitecaps, but without the wind that creates them back in the organic realm, as if I am sitting by a lake while watching an ocean. The bartender is attentive but not overbearing. She comes out from behind the bar and checks on me every twenty minutes.

"You don't have to drink this," she says as she swaps my empty goblet for one filled with a generous ladle of sangria from a fresh batch. "But it's here if you need it."

"Thank you, Sadie," I let her know by my tone that my reading material may warrant another round.

"People usually read for pleasure around here."

"Usually?" I inquire.

"For certain people, work was pleasure, and they see no reason to change."

I nod in tribute to the forthright logic and glance at my list of perverted clues.

"Do you know what an eye loupe is?" I wonder out loud.

"It's a jeweler's eyepiece," she answers. "They use it to inspect gems and stones."

"Ah," I consider what Fiona and her husband may have used it for. The loupe shares a line item with a pair of tweezers and a jar of plum sauce, which opens up a slew of possibilities.

"Flag me down if you need anything else," Sadie says before heading back to her post. "Refills, appetizers…research."

We trade nonchalant salutes.

I bury myself in the list for a spell before taking yet another break to stare out at the ocean. I hear myself comment on how beautiful it is, which is odd, because that does not align with my thoughts, which concern how peaceful the ocean can look while teeming with drama and tension below its surface.

Then I hear myself greet Sadie.

I sneak a glance backwards. I cannot see the full bar, as my line of sight is not directly in front of the window facing out toward the patio, but I can see half of Devin take a seat. Much to my surprise, I am glad to see him, until I see all of Phil take a seat next to the unobscured half of Devin.

He told me how much he liked Phil, which implied they were spending time together, which failed to bother me because the focus was on the greatness of Phil. Seeing them together at the same bar where Phil and I first met detonates the serenity I had managed when their relationship was an abstraction, a line in an equation proving our mutual admiration for a joint friend.

I mutter questions asking how much is too much, why poaching my friend was not enough, and what is really driving the decision to steal our island getaway on top of everything else, all the while pretending to concentrate on the list as I wait for Sadie to come over and check on me. I try to eavesdrop on their conversation, but my agitation fills the space between us and drowns the enunciation of their words, reducing them to noise. I would beckon Sadie over, but if I turn around to make that move, Devin or Phil may spot me, so I sit and simmer, my frustration stewing to a boil that keeps me from not only hearing them, but hearing Sadie when she arrives.

"Mr. Orr?" she startles me. "Sorry."

"No, no," I regroup. "I was just lost in my thoughts."

"You have a twin at the bar."

"You didn't tell him I'm here?" I hope.

"No."

"Thank you."

"Is he responsible for the two of you dying?" she tries to understand my determination to avoid him.

"We're not actually twins."

"Oh," she assesses the situation. "Is he your clone?"

"Yes," I pounce. "I made him so I could multitask and send him to hang out with people I don't really want to hang out with."

"Phil seems nice."

"He is," I acknowledge. "I like spending time with him. Very much. But I have this work I need to do, this list I need to take care of, and I didn't want to hurt Phil's feelings. It's the afterlife. It's all about fun and leisure and adventure. I couldn't tell him I need to get some work done instead of spend time with him."

"A clone comes in handy."

"It sure does. But every once in a while we cross paths."

"That is awkward," she sympathizes.

"Maybe you could help me out."

"Anything."

I take a deep breath and hope to be forgiven by the executive board, or whatever office the higher power might occupy.

"I need to clap your ears," I decide to be transparent.

"What?"

"You know..." I act out the maneuver on an imaginary head.

"What for?"

"So I can become you."

She contemplates the request.

"Okay," she agrees. She is a projection in my simulation, after all.

"I'll try my best to bring you back. If not here, then some other bar or restaurant I imagine."

"I'm curious to see if part of me will still be inside this body, riding around with you."

"Let me know, if we meet again."

"I will."

She leans over, offering a clear path to her ears. I place my goblet on the notepad to keep my list from blowing away, in case the transformation creates any turbulence, though I am certain it does not.

I sneak a peek at the bar to make sure neither Devin nor Phil are watching. They are too deep in conversation to notice anything around them.

"Thank you, Sadie."

"No," she insists. "Thank you. This might be interesting."

"I hope it is."

The takeover seems to take place before I complete the clap. I am leaning over in front of the empty chair I was sitting in.

As with my occupation of the party boy at the arena, I still feel like me, but look different. I put my hands on my new breasts, but I feel my chest, as if my hands went through a hologram of the breasts to reach my chest. I am clutching them, though. I look down to make sure. Then I look around to make sure no one is watching me grapple with the breast-chest paradox. Nobody is, so I check the situation in my crotch and reach the same impasse. I become so fascinated by what I see versus what I feel that I approach the bar much later than Sadie would have if she was still driving this vehicle.

Before I put my ride into gear, I notice the notepad trapped under the sangria goblet. I tear out the pages I need, fold them into my pocket, and take a sheepish lap around the patio, nodding at the occasional occupied table before repositioning myself behind the bar.

Devin and Phil are discussing an angle of the afterworld Phil and I never touched on.

"If someone can change who they are, then what was that all about on the earthly plane?" Devin asks him.

"Spoken like someone who had a great life on earth," Phil aims right for the privilege.

"Let's say they find happiness as another person," Devin proceeds as if accustomed to the accusation. "Is the happiness really theirs?"

"What if they had a disability on earth?"

"That's different. They're not changing who they are."

"But those challenges were a part of who they were, in some cases a major part. By erasing them, according to you, they're cheating."

"You're assuming they want to erase them."

"Good reminder," Phil acknowledges before something occurs to him. "Do we know anyone who had a disability on earth?"

"I don't."

"Me neither. Nobody who's hear yet."

"Too bad," Devin takes a sip of whatever sits in his highball glass. "It would be so convenient if we could ask one person to speak for an entire group of people."

"We change in all sorts of ways after we arrive here," Phil stands by his point. "Look at you. Would you have been the least bit concerned with people who aren't like you back on earth?"

"Maybe."

"Even if they weren't invested in your company?"

"No."

"There you go," Phil seizes the admission in spite of its jokey tone. "If we can change our attitude, change our perspective, why can't we change our bodies?"

"Whose afterlife is it at that point?"

"On the inside they're still the same."

"I'll say," I let slip.

They stop and look at me.

"Sorry," I bow and drift farther down the bar from them. "Didn't mean to interrupt."

"Not a problem," Phil assures me.

"Could you freshen this up?" Devin taps his glass.

"Certainly," I spring into service before a realization hits. "Remind me what you're having, sir?"

"Aw, Sadie," he sounds peeved, but might be kidding. "I thought we were friends."

I try to think of a favorite drink he may have had, but my relationship to his memories has been fading since my return to earth last year, and favorite drink is a low priority.

"Just tell her," Phil wishes.

"Cuba Libre," Devin grants.

"What?" Phil calls him out for changing his answer.

"Of course," I ignore Phil's reaction and tap my head in faux punishment in honor of the customer always being right.

I have no recollection of Devin ever drinking a Cuba Libre, and have no knowledge of the recipe.

"If you'll excuse me, gentlemen," I say. "I need to restock the ingredients. You cleaned us out, Mr. Orr!"

"I don't need premium rum," he smirks. "The well is fine. And heavy on the Coke."

"Okay," I exhale with relief at being bailed out, and inhale anxiety over the probability he is on to me.

"What did you mean?" Phil asks as I start to free Cuba with rum and Coke.

"About what?" I stall as I replenish Devin's drink.

"When you said 'I'll say' after I said people would still be the same on the inside."

"She's a projection," Devin snags his glass as I finish filling it. "She was being agreeable."

"And because I'm a projection, I know physical changes around here are truly only skin deep. It's not even skin."

Devin is further annoyed by the help.

"You've played multiple people?" Phil asks.

"I have," I confirm. "And no matter what I look like, I always feel like me."

"Whatever you are," Devin grumbles.

"Devin..." Phil scolds him.

"He's right," I intercede on Devin's behalf. "I don't know what I am. I've been a hundred different people, and it feels like a distraction from knowing what's underneath."

As fun as it is to annoy him, compliance is the best way to be part of the conversation.

"My point exactly," Devin warms up. "If a projection finds no value in physical change, why would a human being?"

"Because human beings know who they are," Phil says.

He looks at me.

"Sorry, Sadie. I only mean that in the biological sense."

"It's a fair point," I assure him.

"We're just as lost when it comes to knowing who we are in the spiritual sense."

His concern for the feelings of a projection makes me all the more grateful for the chance to speak with him again, if only for a minute, incognito.

"How long have you been Sadie?" he asks.

I try to hide how much the question takes me by surprise.

"Yes," Devin takes a keen interest in my response. "How long, exactly?"

"Well," I hedge. "You know how time is here."

"True," Phil commiserates.

"What are some other parts you've played?" Devin asks.

"They usually don't have names," I draft an answer. "Just faces in a crowd. This is the rare opportunity to have more of an identity."

"Such self-awareness," Devin mock-marvels. "I've never had such an enlightening talk with a projection, even the ones with a name tag."

"This must be what you want, then," I say. "Our job is to serve you."

"I have Phil. I don't need a projection to have a fulfilling conversation."

"The more, the merrier," Phil shrugs into his powers of mediation.

"Thank you, Phil," I swerve into the space he has provided. "Can I get you a refill?"

"A refill," Devin crafts a play on words. "That's what I need. A re-Phil. A do-over with my friend Phil, where we can hang out with no interruptions."

"You're right," I nod and back up.

"Actually I would like a refill," Phil focuses on the initial question. "In the true sense of the word."

He offers an apologetic smile on behalf of his drinking buddy.

"Gin and tonic," he informs me before I have to ask.

"There isn't a cute nickname for it you'd like to use instead?" I poke Devin without looking at him.

"G and T?" Phil reaches for one.

"That's not very cute," Devin scoffs.

"Saves me one syllable," Phil shrugs.

"About time for me to take a lap," I announce as I finish mixing a drink for Phil while maintaining a lack of eye contact with Devin. "If you'll excuse me."

"With pleasure," Devin quips.

I hear Phil sigh and gin up a rebuke.

Their bickering falls short of a volume I can make out as I make my way toward the sea, to the patio. Since the simulation is mine, I insure no customer asks me for anything so I can walk and ponder rather than serve. I pass the table where I sat in my original form and consider bussing my half-full goblet of sangria, but decide instead to chug the rest and leave the empty behind. I reach the edge of the patio and find a spot that faces the ocean out of sight from the bar, in case Devin wants to confront me, which proves to be the case after fifteen seconds of salty air and choppy surf.

"I wonder if a person can file stalking charges in the afterlife," he asks aloud.

"This is my simulation," I remind him. "Not yours. I understand that must be difficult for you to grasp, that something of mine is not yours."

"Full circle," he concedes.

"How did you even find this place?"

"You opened it up, and we have that thing between us. It sounded nice, even though I knew you'd be here."

"Maybe because I'd be here."

"I was curious what it would be like," he admits. "I figured weird. Though not this weird..."

He gestures at my current appearance.

"How soon could you tell?" I ask.

"Right away," he grins.

"We have that thing," I borrow his phrase.

"We do."

"Then why act like such a misogynist pig toward me?"

"Drop the sexism, please. I told you I knew right away you weren't a real woman. The woman you're wearing isn't even a real woman."

"Okay then. Why such a jerk?"

Chauvinism now off the table, he considers my question in earnest.

"Overcompensating," he decides. "Trying too hard not to give away your game."

"I think you wanted to wag Phil in my face."

"Maybe," he allows.

"Or maybe you resent me."

"Why would I resent *you*?"

He lands so hard on the word 'you' that I feel like lashing out.

"My power exceeds yours now," I taunt. "On both ends, here and there, and you can't stand it."

"I'm in paradise. Power doesn't mean anything here."

"It didn't until you made a clone of yourself."

"So you do remember whose life you're living," he claps back.

"I've got my own identity now," I keep the pressure on. "Sponsored by a level of upper management nobody ever gets to meet."

"Your identity is defined by not having one. You're more of a spirit than a person."

"Is that supposed to be an insult?"

"I don't know," he yields and broods. "We got along so well last time."

My memory of that last encounter is likewise a fond mix, so I lay down my arms as well and fill the lull between us with a touch of remorse.

"Could I ask you for an insane favor?" I come up with a way to put our newfound bond back together again, or maybe destroy it. "And I don't mean insane as a slang term. I mean certifiably mad."

"You could," he wades into an answer. "But I reserve the right to refuse based on the level of insanity."

"Fair enough," I agree and flounder for a way to word my request.

"Well?" he waits.

I decide it best to simply spill it.

"Can you check to see if I have balls?"

He regards me with a calm I did not anticipate, which is soothing at first, then drags into unease.

"I can feel them," I suppose an explanation is in order. "Even though they don't appear to be there. It's like I can reach through this body I'm in and touch my own, like this body is a visual shroud, a hologram..."

"A projection?"

"Yes," I consent. "I've been trying to come up with something of my own, but can't quite get there."

"Sure," he steps forward. "I'll check."

"Thanks," I brace myself.

"Promise you won't call Human Resources?"

"Just do it."

He does.

"Nope," he concludes. "You have no balls. And I mean that only in the physical, literal sense."

"Nice of you to clarify."

"When it comes to metaphorical, figurative balls, you have lots of them. Great big ones. You're based on me, after all."

"Yes I am. Now would you please remove your hand?"

Devin smiles and holds on a second before complying.

"Hey there," Marlowe appears beside us, like a boxing referee going over the rules with a pair of fighters before a match. He has ditched the fedora and trench coat in favor of a hatless ensemble featuring a v-neck sweater with a collared shirt underneath.

"Hello, Marlowe," I greet him as one colleague to another passing in the corridor. "I don't imagine you've met Devin."

"No," he acknowledges and shakes his hand.

"Devin," I caption their shake. "This is Marlowe, the administrator I've been working with. Marlowe, this is Devin, my lab sample."

"More like inspiration," Devin brushes off my jab as they stop shaking.

"To what do we owe the pleasure?" I ask Marlowe.

"When you laid hands on each other, I figured it might be a good time to intervene."

"Is that why you went with the family therapist look?" I reference his wardrobe.

"Could be..." he looks down at his outfit and thinks it through.

"No worries," Devin contributes. "We were bonding after a brief rough spot in our relationship. It was consensual."

Marlowe glances at me for confirmation.

I offer it with a nod.

"The interior-exterior body paradox?" Marlowe guesses.

"Takes some getting used to," I verify.

"You may never," he cautions. "You're the first human with the ability to take it this far."

I turn to Devin.

"Don't say I'm not human," I anticipate his input.

He holds up his hands in exaggerated innocence.

"We morph into all kinds of human figures," Marlowe continues. "But without human bodies of our own to cover, we don't experience the paradox like you do."

"I plan to use it sparingly."

"Just to play tricks on me," Devin chirps.

"Is that why you're in the same simulation again?" Marlowe asks.

"I was here first," I defend myself.

"That sounds juvenile," Devin says.

"It's true," I say it more to Marlowe. "No matter how it sounds. I came here to study for the mockup Trisha gig that Devin suggested."

"The what?"

"Do you want to describe it?" I ask Devin. "Or should I?"

He answers me by answering Marlowe.

"If a requirement of working for you is that he has to work for Trisha," he explains to him, "then he needs to know what that's going to be like. So I encouraged him to gather some intel from the murder victims he came here to find and drive their killer insane with it."

I pull the list from my pocket, unfurl it, and point it at Marlowe.

He squints at the top.

"I see," he may be reading the list, but really seems to be collecting his thoughts.

"My first dirty deed when I get back," I say with pretend pride.

"Aside from impersonating me," Devin says with pretend self-deprecation. "And all the indiscretion that involves."

Marlowe stops pretending to read.

"Could I speak with you alone?" he asks me.

"Of course," Devin pouts. "You two go ahead and strategize. I'll figure things out on the fly if I get sucked into one of your case worker simulations."

"If that happens," Marlowe says. "It will be corrected before you have a chance to do anything."

"A chance to screw up anything," Devin assumes what Marlowe is thinking.

"We appreciate your concern," Marlowe smiles at him and puts his arm around me.

Devin scoffs and heads back to the bar.

"See you around," he says over his shoulder. "Maybe. By accident."

"Go ahead and keep using the sim," I say over my shoulder as Marlowe leads me in the opposite direction toward the sea. "My Maui is your Maui."

Devin raises a thumb while walking away.

I keep an eye on him to see if he adds a turn and a look to compliment the thumb, but he keeps his back to me.

Marlowe keeps pressing me for the few more seconds it takes to reach where the patio meets the shore. He stops us at the edge and lets go.

"How insane are you hoping to drive the man in question?" he turns to face me.

"Best case scenario?" I decide to be upfront. "All the way."

"And you're okay with that?"

"I'm not pulling a trigger, or swinging a blunt object. Just sending some texts."

He looks out at the ocean.

"Do you think Trisha's jobs are going to be that diabolical?" he asks.

"Maybe worse. At least this guy deserves whatever we manage to do to him. She'll probably want dirt on innocent people."

"Not to kill them."

"To ruin them," I refuse to let him excuse her. "Everything I give her will lead to a lot of businesses going under or being taken over."

He nods, his focus still on the ocean I fabricated.

"Is that why you wanted to speak with me one-on-one?" I ask.

"No," he swings into a sly eagerness that would fit better under a fedora than above the v-neck. Plus the fedora would provide protection from the sun. He wants me to ask him about what he is so excited to say, but his wardrobe gets in my way.

"Would you like to switch to an outfit that suits the setting?" I ask instead. "Maybe shorts and an aloha shirt?"

"I'm fine," he insists. "I don't sweat."

"Okay, then. Let's hear it. What exactly did you want to talk to me about?"

His fading concern over being in league with Trisha fades even faster. He positions himself as though standing at a podium.

"We think we found a way to communicate with you on earth," he twinkles.

"Who's 'we'?"

"My fellow administrators and me."

"Ah."

"Are you disappointed?"

"Just curious."

"Always looking to climb to the next level," he grouses with a head shake.

"Sorry. But it's hard not to move up and wonder what's even higher up."

"Did you even hear the part about us finding a way to communicate with you on earth?"

"That could come in handy."

"We can use the ghost portals," he reveals.

I try to trace what that means, but fail to camouflage my confusion.

"Management told us they explained ghosts to you," he prods.

"They're, like, a temporary breakthrough," I recall.

"That's right," he confirms. "A rip in the curtain between worlds. We tried out a fair number of those rips, and it looks like we can treat them like speakerphones."

"That must have been interesting for the people on the other side."

"We made sure it wasn't traumatic for them."

"How?" I find that hard to believe.

"We only used a portal when the ghost wasn't making an appearance and only used our voices."

"Hearing voices. Nothing traumatic about that."

"We grounded them in reality. We would tell someone passing by that we were hiding because we ripped our pants, and then ask them for the location so we could call a friend to bring us a new pair of pants."

I imagine those situations playing out.

"It beats trying to sync up with the ghost," he defends their method. "Ghosts are just a loop, a recording of the resident before they were whisked back to the afterworld. Trying to talk over that would be way more unsettling."

"Did any of the pedestrians strike up a conversation?" I ignore the weirdness scale he has invented.

"Not many. We accounted for the possibility as part of our preparation. We asked the residents who carved out the portals we used why they did it, what inspired them, so we could adopt their stories, their ghost stories, if we needed to keep the bit going longer."

"Oh yeah? What was yours?"

"I had a man who restored an old car and got ripped off by a smog technician who took a bribe to pass it but instead reported the crime so he could try to swipe the car for himself. When my guy found out, he drove in a rage to confront the smog man and spun out into a river on the way. He was still so irate when he crashed, way more than he was scared, that he managed to hold on for a moment before the crossover pulled him into the afterlife and left a mark. All his ghost does is pace the riverbank and scream obscenities."

"I hope he's found some peace in the afterlife."

"He's doing much better, but looking forward to making an appointment with the smog technician when his time comes."

"Did you have to use any of that?"

"The lady I spoke with was very sweet and didn't ask any questions. I was a little disappointed. I had done my homework and was ready to play the part. I asked if she had heard of the ghost that supposedly haunts the riverbank."

"Had she?"

"No. She's not a regular on the river trail, and the ghost isn't out there very often. But she seemed delighted to hear from me. I think she was happy to have a story to tell."

He shifts his position, and with it the tone of our conversation.

"So if our dry runs are any indication," he adds a transitional phrase, "all I need from you is a convenient haunted location, and a set day and time when you can check in."

"And you're going to plug that in to your calendar?" I razz him.

"We'll use the portals to keep track. We may not have a sense of time, but we're not idiots."

"Well," I let him think I may be pondering their idiocy while I sift for any supernatural legends I may have heard about my adopted town. "There's an old hotel that was renovated not too long ago, and on the occasional slow news day when there aren't any neighborhood tragedies to report on, the local news outlet likes to broadcast a story about a ghost that's supposed to wander the halls. Maybe it's just promotion for the grand re-opening."

"Would a ghost be something to brag about if you're trying to attract people?"

"There aren't a whole lot of reasons to visit our town."

"What kind of ghost?"

"I don't know. Does it matter?"

"I may want to contact the resident who made it."

"A little girl, I think. Maybe I'm getting my stories crossed. That seems so typical."

"Little ghost girls are popular," he confirms. "Built-in tragic backstory. Much more compelling than a middle-aged car buff."

I feel for the notepad and pen Sadie has in her apron and pull it out as if taking an order.

"Shall we say the first Monday of the month at two in the afternoon?" I suggest as I write down the name and location of the hotel. "That should be a pretty dead time of day."

"Good, because you'll need to walk around and call out to me."

I stop writing.

"We don't know the layout of the hotel," he explains. "Or where our resident's loop appears in it."

I start writing again with a prolonged groan.

"Only the first time," he assures me. "After that, we'll know the routine."

"Can I call out to you in a whisper?"

"Maybe somewhere in between. A loud whisper."

I tear the paper from the pad and flap it in front of him.

"Just the first time," he reminds me.

When he reaches for the bait, I yank it back.

"Yes?" he correctly supposes there is one condition.

"Who was the woman at the football game?"

"I need more information," he genuinely does not know what I am referring to.

"Feathered hair, baggy mom jeans, thousand-yard stare. Sitting in the stands when I checked on Cam Lamp."

"A friend of his, maybe?"

"She's not a woman," I correct myself. "She's a projection, but hard to think of as a projection thanks to her stunning level of self-awareness."

"Ah," he realizes. "So that's the look they went with."

"They?"

"As you know, our team here is gender fluid. I think that's what you'd call it. Species fluid, come to think of it."

"What were they doing there?

"Spying."

"Spying?"

"Or trying to. How hard can it be to imitate a projection?" he acts as though the colleague is in front of him for a debriefing. "All you have to do is sit there, and if a resident asks questions, agree with them. Or better yet, shut up and pretend you're strictly a background model."

"What do you think I'm capable of?" I pull him back into a conversation with me.

"This is new to all of us," he squirms. "Not just you."

"I heard that last time I was here, too. How much damage can I do?"

"Nothing, really, in the grand scheme. If a resident has a problem with something you do, they complain to management, and we're in charge of management, so we're pretty well-insulated from anything going higher up, which I know must be hard for you to hear."

"Then why spy?" I ignore his dig.

"We're excited," he admits. "And consequently a little curious."

I extend the paper his way and let him take it this time.

"I have some pages of my own I still need to study," I reach for an exit. "And I'd like to get out from under this Sadie suit before I'm expected to mix anymore drinks."

"Remember you can only do that by entering a new simulation."

"Oh," I pretend to be reminded. "That's right."

I suspect I may have overplayed the part, but Marlowe takes no offense, or does some pretending of his own. I nearly ask him which it is when something else occurs to me.

"Will Sadie take this back after I leave?"

"Yes."

"We were hoping to compare notes on the experience."

"She won't have any notes. She'll make some up if you come back and ask."

"She's a projection," I recognize the situation with a sigh.

"Where are you off to now?" he joins me in looking for a way out.

"I really like the pool where Aunt Gladys rents her condo."

"Don't let her catch you there," he repeats the rule.

"A non-issue," I assure him. "I'm pretty certain Devin has ruined that relationship, and I'm in no position to repair it."

He laughs.

"What?" I ask.

"You really are perfect for the job."

"I haven't taken it yet."

He reaches out for a hand shake. I think of reasons to explain why I cannot yet commit.

"Next time we talk," he clarifies the purpose of the hand shake, "it'll probably be through the portal."

I take his hand now that I know it only represents a goodbye.

"If I can figure out how to work it," I kid.

"It's not a new cell phone. All you have to do is call my name and listen for my voice."

He smiles and disappears.

I turn around and find myself standing next to a pool. I look at my reflection on the surface of the water and see myself rather than Sadie. The pool is in a courtyard surrounded by condominiums. It may not be the same complex where Gladys lives, but as far as I can recall, it appears to be a close replica, and exactly what I need to focus on taking the lovers' list to heart.

The water is clean and free of swimmers, the patio furniture likewise deserted, and aside from sporadic clusters of purple agapanthus springing from squares of dirt that dot the pavement around the perimeter, no plant or wildlife to distract me. The hum of the pool filter is the only sound I hear as I settle into a lightweight chaise lounge and reacquaint myself with the chaise lounge with the hole in it that Fiona and her husband used for whatever hijinks that later excited her lover upon hearing about it, maybe more so than her husband while experiencing it.

I have no doubt their lounge chair, even with the hole in it, was far nicer than the one I am sitting in. I make my way through the other items on the list, coming up with mnemonics to remember them. Some are easier than others. The vampire teeth, for example, serve as a clear-cut symbol of the husband out for blood; the vinyl body pillow imprinted with photos of raw meat represent how he perceived his wife; and the toe-shaped dildos, should I include them, feed into any old slang term about kicking ass, or maybe even putting his foot in his mouth, depending on how they used them. But others are more elusive, and none stand out as being any more outlandish, or any more random, so I cannot apply a scale of absurdity. It reads less like a list of hallmarks from a series of high-end erotic romps, and more like a scavenger hunt scheduled to take place in a strip mall anchored by a Dollar Tree and a Party City. Tropical fruit swirl mini roll-ups are as arbitrary as a red rubber rain slicker, but at least I can categorize those two together as things more associated with childhood than adulthood. How is a yellow mesh safety vest any more memorable than an artificial grass doormat? And did they ever have sex without props?

The surroundings keep their distance from pulling me away from my studies, but when I look up and around to clear my head, or by chance spot an object that may trigger a trick that locks in one of the items, I think of how fun it would be to have Gladys here. I conjure up a projection of her to see how the universe may interpret my request, and find the results demonstrate why projections may be fine for the company of strangers, but lacking when trying to impersonate someone familiar.

For starters, she enters the courtyard from the wrong direction, on the opposite side from where her building is located. Then she says "so nice to see you," which is the last thing Gladys would say in that situation. She would instead make a wise crack about trespassing, or avoiding her, probably both. When the projection asks me what I am doing, and I tell her what I am memorizing, she says "how interesting," which is even further out of character than the greeting. Gladys would bask in the depravity of the task, insist I read the list aloud, and howl with laughter that builds after every line. I tell her about the two jobs I am considering, working for competing forces with one foot in each world, and rather than giving me her honest opinion, the projection says she trusts me to make the right decision. When I ask her how to do that, she tells me to follow my heart.

Her standard questions and conventional answers grow so tiresome I am grateful when cracks split the pavement and fan out across the courtyard, water churns and rolls over the sides of the pool, the ground opens beneath me, and I am swallowed by a familiar sensation of falling while holding still, suspended between the pit and the sky that brightens for a blinding moment before all light snaps into a yawning darkness that does not hide anything because everything is gone. I drop through all of that nothing without moving until it feels more like sinking. My body rotates into the prone position, and with a mattress at my back I hear the sound of voices but no words.

I assume Trisha will be one of the first persons I see. I want to thank her for making me more than a projection, for not being so agreeable, for the chance to develop character. Devin had input, but it was her execution.

What appears to be another successful return trip from beyond convinces me that taking the job is inevitable, and probably always was. My hesitation was a performance, a stall tactic to create some leverage. There are still conditions to discuss, so rather than telling her how grateful I am for the ability to take a stand, I decide to express my gratitude by showing her how disagreeable I can be.

# Chapter Nine

Other people may be in the room when I wake up, but I cannot say for sure because all I can see is Trisha hovering a foot above my face.

"Well?" she asks.

"Nice to see you, too, Trisha."

"Oh, please," she leans back to allow for arm gestures. "We both know why we're here."

With the wave of her arms I can see that we are in fact the only two in what looks like a medical examination room. I am laid out on the padded table with the section beneath my back propped up, wearing what I was wearing on the day I left.

"Was that really two weeks?"

"Did you go there or not?"

Being absorbed in the afterlife had me casting aside the many alarming reservations about working with her. Whatever thrill the prospect of working with Marlowe provided during my stay is fading fast in the glare of her face. The lie stirs. I get ready to tell it. But also stirring is my unexpected soft spot for Cam Lamp, and the kind of person he may represent in this life or the other. The kind of person Marlowe wants to help, that I want to help. I want to know if she really is just using him to stamp my passport, or if she has plans for anyone close to him who is still living. I play groggy and weigh my options, wondering if the situation has to be one way or the other: telling the truth and working for her, or lying and leaving her behind. I talk myself into a third way: telling the truth and leaving her behind.

"Your mother killed him."

"Ha!" she exalts. "I knew it!"

"What does that mean? Why are you so happy? Was Cam that bad?"

"Not at all," she rocks in her chair as if doing so may extend the glow. "I always liked Cam. Even if he should have gone by Cameron."

"You don't seem to mind he was murdered."

"By my *mother*," she emphasizes. "I can't wait until the next time she asks me for money."

She stands up and paces around, her scarves and crepe holding on to keep up with her.

"I want to call her so badly," she plots aloud. "But waiting for her to call me will taste so much sweeter. How did she do it?"

I should sit up to reveal the facts of the case, out of respect for Cam, but cannot overcome the feeling of being reclined.

"She pinned his arms under the pretense of dominant-submissive sex, fed him a large bite of flourless chocolate torte, then crammed it down his windpipe with her tongue."

She thinks through the logistics.

"Why didn't he chew her tongue off?" she asks.

"Too busy gasping for breath, I imagine."

"See why I want to have nothing to do with her? She was bad enough before adding murder to the list of terrible things she does to people."

"Are you going to turn her in?"

"With what evidence?"

"How are you going to explain to her that you know?"

"I'll tell her I hired a private investigator. Maybe tell her Donnie chased down the story for me. She was always creeped out by Donnie."

"You sure she won't kill Donnie then?"

"Verbal and mental abuse are more her speed," she settles back into her chair. "They last longer. More fun. Death by cake is bound to be her limit. I can't see her using any standard weapons to murder someone."

"I guess that's good news for Cam's son."

"You think it was about Cam's will?"

"Don't you?"

"Never thought about it," she shrugs. "I had enough of my own money when they met."

"I could have asked him," I search her for any signs of compassion. "But after I got what I needed for your sake, I decided to leave him alone."

"Ah," she nods.

I wait for her to ask why I left him alone, but she is too busy with her own thoughts.

"He was in a bad place," I provide my answer anyway.

"Hell?"

"No."

"That's good," she cackles. "I was about to say, you didn't have to go there on my account."

I want to describe the pain he was in over leaving his son behind before being able to reconcile, and how if I asked about the will, I would only be making it worse, since money can only be wrapped around a wound so many times.

"You'd have to really want the job," she keeps riding her crack about hell.

Nothing Marlowe can offer would mitigate the damage she is determined to inflict. Nobody will deserve what she has in mind for them. The status quo between before and after must be maintained. I wish I had lied, pretended I was nowhere but unconscious for two weeks. The only alibi I can muster for my honesty is that it left no doubt as to whether I should work for her.

"About that..." I say.

"The job?"

"Yes."

"When can you start?" she asks.

I am in no condition to match wits with her, already one bad decision in debt thanks to a hasty insistence on the truth.

"I'd like a few days to adjust," I buy some time. "Reacquaint myself with earth. Then a few more days to speak with my attorney."

"About what?"

"What happens when I'm away for all those extended periods."

"Whatever happened this time. That's what happens."

"Have you met my attorney?" I try to humor my way into the extra days. "Or more to the point, fought through the pain of speaking with him on the phone? It leaves an impression."

"I'll give you the few days to adjust," she reaches into her wrap to produce my phone. "If you want to squeeze in anything else while you're adjusting, be my guest."

I take the phone.

"Your ride is in the lobby," she puts out our conversation. "We'll let her know you're on your way."

She buries herself in a phone of her own while I engage my muscles to rise from the examination table. After a couple of faulty steps, I find my stride and make it to the door upright.

I pause before opening it.

"Is there anything else you'd like to know about where I've been?" I ask her.

She looks up from her screen, but not at me, to think about it.

"No," she decides in seconds and looks in my direction. "Not particularly. Is there anything you'd like to tell me about it?"

"There is no hell. But you have to face the people you've wronged."

She smiles.

"Nobody ever knows it's me."

The smile drops as she re-enters her screen.

Saying good bye seems pointless, so I walk into the hall and wonder which way to go. I look to the left, then to the right, when I hear a voice spray "psst" from the left where I was just looking.

The female half of the two suits who haunt the company now stands at the end of the corridor, gesturing for me to walk toward her. When I am halfway there, she holds up her hand as a silent command to halt. I obey. She points to my right. I turn to see a door marked "stairs". Before I enter, she sprays another "psst" and when I look at her, she points downward.

I enter the stairwell and walk down two flights to the first floor. I exit to find myself at the far end of the lobby. Kelly is sitting on a bench by the front door facing the front desk, expecting to see me appear from that direction. I am tempted to spew a "psst" of my own, but walk toward her instead.

About a dozen steps away from her, she notices me, jumps up, and approaches as though she may want to hug. I extend my hand for a shake, imploring her with my eyes to accept it. She deciphers the signal and agrees to my terms.

"Thank you for agreeing to pick me up," I say at high volume as we shake hands.

"I was able to carve out some time in my schedule," she plays along.

We walk out together and as we reach the parking lot, I explain while continuing to face forward, adjusting to the warmth of real sunshine.

"I don't want them to think we have a strong connection. For your own safety, you need to keep your distance from all of this."

She keeps quiet until we are inside her car.

"I thought you were going to lie to her," she says.

"I liked Cam Lamp. I felt sorry for him. Then when I came back and was face-to-face with Trisha, I felt protective of him. I thought seeing how she reacted to what I learned would help my decision."

"And now you don't have a decision," she sighs.

"I can get out of it," I try to convince myself. "I've got a few days to come up with an excuse. Let's get going before their cameras zoom in and read our lips."

"You hungry?" she starts the engine.

"Famished."

"Let's reintroduce Devin to the valley lunch crowd."

"I appreciate the offer, but can we just hit a franchise with large portions of bland food?"

"And no former frenemies hanging around?" she backs out of the spot.

"An added bonus."

She straightens out and shifts into drive.

"What about Dad?" she asks as we move forward. "Did you like him, too?"

Her casual manner in bringing up the subject makes it no less challenging to address.

"You're assuming he was there," I try to be as casual.

"I've been bracing myself for the answer since you've been gone."

"Are you sure you want to do this while you drive?"

"I would prefer it," she reaches the exit and waits for an opportunity to join the rush. "Gives me a chance to compose myself before we enter the restaurant."

I wait until she is on the road and caught up with the flow of traffic.

"I liked your dad most of all," I tell her.

She keeps her eyes on the road as they fill with tears.

"And he loves you very much," I add.

Her tears run out of room and run down her cheeks.

"Way more than your sister," I take a chance on levity.

She rewards the effort with a quick laugh, though she keeps to herself for the rest of our ride to my feeding.

Not until we are seated with our ice waters and waiting for our orders in a booth enclosed by high backs and simulated stained-glass dividers does she revisit the reason we are here.

"Was it a contract murder?"

"It was."

"Who ordered it?"

"I'd rather not tell you."

"Are you afraid I'll do something stupid?"

"Something stupid has already been set in motion to avenge him."

"Are you a part of it?"

"I am, but I'm in no danger. If that matters."

Her eyes sharpen with offense. I dull them with a grin that assures her I was kidding, or maybe curious to see if she does care, and relieved to find she does. She consents to whatever explanation she projects onto my grin and settles back into her sad reflection.

"Did it have to do with money?" she asks.

I hesitate and she takes advantage of the opening.

"Was it about a woman?"

Her father said he wanted me to tell the truth, which I realize now was easier for him to say than for me to do. I subconsciously count to three and jump into his wish ahead of any second thoughts.

"Yes," I land with a splash that I try to keep small.

"She must have been the wife or mistress of someone powerful."

"She was."

"Someone he met through the fascist wealth management program?"

"An old high school flame, believe it or not, who married the wrong person."

"And had an affair with the wrong person."

I wince on behalf of her father.

"Sorry," she softens. "I love my Dad. Very much. But I suspect she wasn't the only one. And I suspect Mom suspects, too."

"Your Dad and this particular woman are actually quite happy together."

"The husband took her out too, eh?"

"He did."

She takes a sympathetic breath.

"He'll blow it with her eventually," she pities the late Fiona. "He couldn't stay with one woman for a year, much less an eternity."

"That's the thing about the afterlife," I decide to join her party. "You can go anywhere and do anything, but you can't escape who you are."

"I assume sex plays a big part in paradise?"

I choose from an overwhelming number of ways I can say that it does.

"It's a bathhouse."

"Then I'm sure Dad is very happy there."

I admire her candor.

"He's got a doozy of a conversation with your mother coming," I feed it.

"I don't know. She might just grab a towel of her own."

"That would fit a pattern."

"Really?" she enjoys our complicity.

"Pretty much everyone I meet there might as well live in a swingers community. Your dad and his girlfriend actually do."

"Sounds like she's no monogamist, either."

"Well," I realize I may have said too much. "They keep to themselves for the most part."

"Then what's the point of living in that community?"

I debate whether I should tell her.

"What?" she digs into my pause.

I use her curiosity as a cue to follow through.

"I don't know how many of them are from your father's side..."

"Oh my..." she covers her mouth.

"See?" I admonish both of us. "This is why I need to limit how much I reveal."

"His parents are still alive," she pursues the matter. "That means..."

"Great grandma and great grandpa."

"Gee Ma and Gee Pa."

"Gees for life."

"I barely knew them."

"That's what everybody says after one of their parties."

"I remember Gee Ma died first. Then when Gee Pa died about two weeks later, everyone said it was because of a broken heart."

"That's sweet."

She looks at me with a smirk, daring me to say what both of us are thinking.

"But now you know it's because he was horny," I take her up on it.

She keeps her laughter as quiet as she can to avoid causing a scene.

"I'm not sure I want to go there now," she catches her breath. "Is it possible to pass on passing over?"

"It's what you make it. Devin has a great aunt who lives by herself and works for a waste management company."

"Like on site at a dump?"

"Yes."

"But still a younger, sexier version of herself."

"No," I pay my respects. "If she has that version of herself in her past, she doesn't use it. A rare bird in the afterworld."

She imagines the afterlife of Aunt Gladys and smiles, then trains her smile on me.

"Thank you," she says.

"I had my reasons for going, too."

"I know, but still. There's plenty of risk involved, way beyond dealing with my dead lusty family members. Lots of variables and danger. I'm very grateful."

"So am I. If it weren't for you, I never would have gone back."

I raise my glass of ice water and we toast.

She wants to know more about the afterlife, of course, and she has earned the right, so I tell her about creating our own environments. I use the home her father helped build as an example, with its lemur butlers and pelican fishing buddies. I explain the way people get in touch with one another. In describing how invitations and simulations operate, I realize the system plays into being with one friend at a time, if any at all, as I cannot imagine many groups of any size agreeing on what to do when each member can star in an infinite number of their own options. I compare making friends on my first trip to watching them spend time with Devin on the second, keeping my distance and thinking how the situation would be an ideal demonstration of the old adage that you can never go back, we are not the same people from that younger episode, and neither are our friends. It would be an ideal demonstration if not for the fact Devin and I really are two different versions of the same person.

I am careful to avoid the revenge plot against the man who murdered her father, and even more careful to never mention Marlowe and the chance to use the afterlife as therapy for the living, since I am certain she would want to help, especially with the wellness program. Involving her would drop Trisha into her life, and I would not be able to live with myself in either dimension if I let that happen.

We delight in knowing when the server delivers our food and refills, she hears us talking about going to Maui or a mixed martial arts match, but does not know the context of our conversation.

"It's nice being able to talk to someone about this," I say.

Or at least most of it.

Kelly bows her head in recognition while folding her paper napkin into a small square that fits in her hand.

"A lot of pressure built up over the past year," I continue. "When I got back from my last trip, all I used it for was to trick people and intimidate them."

"That's on me," she says.

"I gathered it was a lot more on Jalen and Gina."

"I never pushed back on them."

"But you came around."

She twists the paper square and squeezes it.

"Now that I know," she looks at the makeshift stress reliever in her hand. "I kind of hope you do go back."

"It's tempting, isn't it?"

"I can see why you slipped up when talking to Trisha."

"An excuse to leave the door open."

"Let me know if you do. I'll be happy to give you a ride and lend you my ears."

"I will."

The server delivers the bill. Kelly slaps the folder and reels it in.

"You don't have any money on you, anyway," she says as she slides in a card and hands it back to the server.

"You don't have to announce it to everyone," I kid for the benefit of the server, who smiles and assures us she will be right back.

"You're welcome to spend the night," Kelly offers.

"Thank you," I mean it. "But I need to head home and regroup before I even think of an exit strategy."

I also have an errand to run before driving from tech valley to farm valley.

After retrieving my car from Kelly's driveway, I embark on my tour of the three McDonalds locations preferred by the contact Devin provided.

At the first stop I find three potential candidates, each seated in their own booth. They work behind invisible walls made of laptop, phone, and ear buds. Two are heavy and one is thin. All are of indeterminate age, falling anywhere on a wide range of late-twenties to mid-forties. Among the overweight, one is disheveled while the other is groomed. The slender one is disheveled by design.

Since whichever one it is will think I am Devin, I take a slow walk around the rim of the dining room, past their campsites, to see if any of them acknowledge me.

"Again?" the skinny, artfully scruffy one falls for it.

His tech is more streamlined than the setups favored by his thicker contemporaries. All of his devices are small, leaving more space for his large drink, which is the only item purchased from the restaurant.

"Have you eaten?" I offer.

"I don't eat here," he looks at his laptop rather than at me.

"They don't mind?"

"The dining room is never full. Everyone uses the drive-thru or orders online and picks it up."

A reedy, neck-tattooed young man from behind the counter comes by to check on us.

"We're fine," my contact assures him.

They could pass as brothers who wound up on different paths in life. The tech pirate hands the cashier a twenty dollar bill, who then returns to his post at the register.

My contact glares at me, searching for signs of judgment over the exchange. I offer none, which prompts him to proceed.

"Why do you keep coming back every time you need an account?" he asks.

"Why wouldn't I?"

He puffs out a one-syllable laugh.

"I can recycle them?" I reply to his puff.

"You don't know jack shit, do you?"

"About ghost accounts?"

"About any of it. Computers, code. Nothing."

"I wouldn't say that."

"I would."

"That's your opinion."

"That's my price."

"What do you mean?"

"I'll get you another account," he reaches for his phone and holds it up. "But you need to confess, on video, that you are completely and utterly technologically ignorant. That you can barely operate a food delivery app, much less write code. That you were never anything more than a money man with just enough charm to win over enough people who don't know what real charm is."

Which is true in part.

I would grant him the parts about technology and money, but take issue with the part about charm. I was made to overcome that flaw in Original Devin.

I have no interest in building another company when the contract allows it, even if I had the kind of start-up talent that the slight, tousled hacker so disdains. My legacy, as much as it may be mine, lies in charity.

"Do you have a script you want me to follow?" I agree to his terms.

"Oh," he is taken by surprise. "Uh, something like what I said would be fine."

"Okay, then," I sit down in his booth, across the table from him, ready to perform. "Let's do it."

He fumbles for the video app, still adjusting to my willingness.

"We'll do however many takes it takes," he rolls his shoulders and stretches his arms, preparing to raise the phone. "Until I'm satisfied."

I stop responding, saving my breath, waiting for my cue.

He settles in and lines up his shot.

# Chapter Ten

I drive home wondering if am going viral during my two hours on the road. He may keep it for his own personal use, a video to play whenever he needs a boost. But he can have both the emotional support and the vindictive thrill of humiliating Devin by posting it, so that move seems far more likely. I examine myself for the possibility I might also enjoy a public shaming of Devin.

Upon reaching my living room, I conduct an online search for the video but come up empty. Likewise the next morning after I wake up late to a freshly-charged phone. No combination of keywords leads to my McDonalds monologue.

My search provides an excuse to put off my revenge texting. So does messaging my attorney. I use him to kick the haunting even further down the road. I click "Everything" on my contact list and let him know I am back.

His reply reads "ok."

I ask him if he went to Legoland and am pleasantly surprised to receive a "yes." I would ask him how it was, but another "ok" is not going to help me duck responsibility any longer, so I sigh and open my new anonymous account that cost me the low price of Devin's dignity.

I waffle over what kind of written voice I might adopt. Vengeful and harsh? Taunting and playful? My interactions with Fiona in the afterlife offer little insight. She was in such a different place, both literally and figuratively, than she was with her husband. I decide to simply deliver fragments of the list with no personal connective tissue binding them, no narrative voice, the better to keep the message mysterious and avoid mistakes. I send the pieces one at a time, giving each item its own bubble.

"Tapioca"

"Plastic dinosaurs"

"Pool drain"

I stop at three, saving some for later if necessary.

The deed done, I holster my phone and head out for an early lunch.

Sitting at the counter eating a club sandwich and trading small talk with Nita feels better than anything I manufactured in the afterlife. The talk cannot go small enough, the sandwich basic enough. The sound of ice tumbling from her pitcher into my glass when she refills my iced tea may as well be church bells.

My phone vibrates next to my glass.

Not wanting to interrupt my lunch counter rapture, I click on the notification to save the message for later. Retribution can wait.

It quivers again. I click to save.

It quivers again.

And again before I can manage a click.

Again.

I cannot keep up.

It trembles around the counter like a wind-up toy.

"Your phone's really blowing up," Nita notices on her way past. "Big news?"

"Maybe Everything wants to tell me about Legoland after all."

She grins at my joke and I grab the phone as if to whisper at it with intensity to shut up.

It is who I assumed it was.

It is not how I assumed it would proceed.

DARLING!!!

LOVE OF MY LIFE!!!

I KNEW IT!!!

UR ALIVE!!!

WHERE RU????

I KNEW THEY WERE LYING

THEY SAID THEY DID IT

BUT I KNEW THEY WERE LYING

I'M SO HAPPY THEY DIDN'T DO IT!!!!

WHERE RU???
WORST MISTAKE OF MY LIFE
I DIDN'T TELL THEM THAT
BUT I COULD TELL THEY KNEW
THAT'S WHY THEY DIDN'T DO IT
THEY SAVED ME FROM MYSELF
EVEN MORE IMPORTANT
THEY SAVED U!!!
WHERE!!!
ARE!!!
U???
YOU???
I'VE NEVER BEEN SO HAPPY
SO HAPPY SOMEONE DISOBEYED ORDERS
HA HA!!!
AND TO HEAR FROM U!!!
SORRY
YOU!!!
LOVE OF MY LIFE!!!
SO HAPPY!!!
LOVE?
HELLO?
HELLOOOO???
DID THEY SCARE YOU?
THOSE ANIMALS I HIRED
THEY SPARED YOU
BUT DID THEY SCARE YOU?
TELL YOU TO STAY AWAY?
NEVER COME NEAR ME
EVER AGAIN
IS THAT WHAT THEY DID?
WHAT DID THEY SAY???

DID THEY THREATEN YOU???
TELL ME!!!!!!
TALK TO ME MY LOVE
TALK TO ME
MY LOVE
MY DARLING
PLEASE
I CAN MAKE THEM GO AWAY
THEY AREN'T THE ONLY ONES
I KNOW OTHERS
WHO DO WHAT THEY DO
TELL ME WHAT THEY DID
I'M SORRY
I'M SORRY
I NEED TO SAY THAT
I'M SORRY I DIDN'T SAY IT ALREADY
I'M SORRY
FOR NOT SAYING I'M SORRY
SOONER
I SHOULD HAVE SAID IT
RIGHT AWAY
PLEASE FORGIVE ME
MY LOVE
PLEASE FORGIVE ME
I WAS SO EXCITED TO HEAR FROM YOU
I LOVE YOU
SO MUCH
PLEASE COME BACK
PLEASE
YOU CAN DO WHATEVER YOU WANT
WHEN YOU COME BACK
I JUST WANT YOU HERE

WITH ME
PLEASE
PLEASE
PLEASE
COME BACK
ALL WILL BE FORGIVEN
WHY WON'T YOU REPLY?
WHY DID YOU CONTACT ME?
WHY DO THIS?
WHAT ARE YOU DOING?
ANSWER ME!!!
WHY ARE YOU DOING THIS???
I'M NOT THE ONLY ONE
WHO NEEDS TO APOLOGIZE
I FORGIVE YOU
FOR FUCKING AROUND
FOR BEING A WHORE
FUCKING ME FOR MONEY
FUCKING THAT LOSER
TO FEEL SUPERIOR
TO PRETEND UR BETTER THAN ME
I FOUND U BEFORE
I CAN FIND U AGAIN

The messages stop. My hand continues to buzz even after the phone no longer does. Nita asks me how I am doing. She is referring to my lunch, so I tell her I am fine. Holding the phone in my hand muffled the sound of the alerts, so she does not realize how many messages rolled in, and has forgotten about them.

I wish I could forget them.

Before I sign off for good, I send him three more bubbles.

"Red rubber rain slicker"

"Vampire teeth"

"Toe dildos."

The phone throbs back to life. Another swarm of texts splatters across the screen. I look away and press the button to turn off the phone, holding it down as if leaning against a door the enraged husband is trying to break through, throwing all my weight against his. The phone falls silent. The grunting and pounding are gone. But the source is still lying in wait on the other side, taking a breather, storing energy for the next attempt.

# Chapter Eleven

"I can't do this," I tell Trisha. "I'm sorry."

"Sit down," she offers without looking at me, focusing instead on one of her beachy knickknacks on the coffee table between the couches, a spinning metal whirligig mounted atop a slab of slate with crystals glued to it.

"I'm not staying long," I remain standing behind the couch on my side of the table.

"It probably would be best if you weren't seen here often," she agrees with me. "After today, the only times you have to come to the building are when we send you on a business trip."

"I can't do that."

"You can't do this, you can't do that..."

"All of it," I say. "I can't go back. I won't go back."

She at long last looks at me.

"Why not?" she asks.

"I am thoroughly convinced that an intersection of this life and the afterlife is guaranteed to fail."

"Fail in what sense?"

"It will ruin lives in both worlds."

"I can't speak for the other side," she leans back. "But the lives I'm going to ruin on this side deserve to be ruined."

"According to you."

"Morally reprehensible people who don't deserve what they have," she proceeds as if I said nothing. "If I can't take them over, I'll take their money. Either way, I'm doing them a favor."

"Is that so?"

"They'll be better people in the long run. I'm giving them a chance to figure out who they really are. If they bounce back, they'll have done it on their own. If not, they should never have been in a position of power in the first place, and the world is better off without them."

"Or, more likely, they'll spend all their energy trying to get revenge on you."

"Like I said—"

"They won't know it's you. Yes. Got it. But people will start to notice how much money is rolling your way, how often you benefit from the misfortune of others."

"And by that point they'll know that trying to get revenge on me is a losing proposition."

"Then they'll take out their frustrations some other way, and not in a way that makes the world a better place."

"Oh, come now," she pulls out her phone. "Taking the moral high ground is not compatible with how you were programmed."

She calls up my McDonalds monologue and holds it up for me to see.

"And?" I am curious what she reads into my performance.

"Why did that dirt bag make you do this?" she asks over my lines.

"Why would you assume he's a dirt bag?" I step onto a path of distraction.

"He accepted this as payment," she wiggles the screen as my recital prattles away on it, maintaining her focus. "I suspect you needed access to someone's information, an untraceable account, a way to be a ghost in the machine and follow through on the real reason you had for wanting to go back to the afterlife, a reason you didn't divulge in our meeting, something other than the existential crisis you pretended to have."

"I'm not pretending anymore," I appeal for mercy. "Something happened this time. Something that makes me not want to go back."

"I don't care," she lowers the screen. "I don't care what happened, or why, or how much you were involved. You can do whatever you want when you're there, or here for that matter, as long as what you do includes getting me what I want. Then feed me the information, and I'll do the rest."

"No," I insist.

She sighs and returns her focus to the whirling doodad on the table.

I suppose she has more to say, but a lengthy silence challenges my assumption.

"I'll show myself out," I move to leave.

"I'll be in touch."

I stop all movement.

"Did you not hear me?"

"I heard you," she refreshes the spinning of the thingamabob with a flick. "But you don't have a choice."

"What do you mean I don't have a choice?"

She looks at neither me nor the gizmo, and instead glares into an empty space between the two.

"I'm not sure how I can put it any more clearly," she says.

"Of course I have a choice."

"Devin was conspicuously absent while you were under."

"That's who he is now," I cling to the script. "He avoids the public eye."

She shifts her gaze from the empty space to me.

"He avoids the public eye by being dead."

I feel like a more sophisticated version of the empty space.

"As I was saying," she turns her attention back to the souvenir artwork and gives it another shove. "I'll be in touch."

"Even if what you said is true," I take a halfhearted stab at denial, "which it isn't, one thing has nothing to do with the other."

"Letting the world know you're a clone who stole the identity of the person who commissioned you, a person who died under very suspicious circumstances, has every single thing to do with your life."

"And yours."

"And mine," she grants. "But not in the way you think, or hope."

"Your circumstances are just as suspicious as mine."

"I know," she concedes again without the slightest concern. "I should never had made you. The public outcry will be deafening. I'll be slapped with ethics violations and lose every license and permit I hold. But after all of that happens, and the masses have moved on to the next great outrage, the calls will start to come in. Not from those who want to work with me, but those calling on behalf of those who want to work with me. And they won't say they want to work with me. They'll ask how I'm doing, if there's any way they can help, because now that they've had a chance to think about what happened, the backlash seems a bit much, a bit unfair. We were all headed in that direction. I just accelerated the timeline. Meanwhile, the investigation and trial of Devin's assistants will start, and that will be far more captivating to the world at large. Then there's you, the clone, the first of your kind, the thing all these other things are about. They won't be able to get enough of you."

"Who are 'they'?"

"Everyone."

The concept of everyone is too big to comprehend, impossible to imagine, but as little as ten percent of everyone, five percent, even one percent carries so much weight that I change the subject, hoping I can avoid the sinking feeling of everyone having an opinion of me.

"Did you try to contact Devin because you wanted to get in touch with him?" I follow up on her investigation. "Or were you hoping to practice your blackmail business model?"

"I was confirming the obvious," she sits back on the couch and treats our exchange like any other conversation.

"You were suspicious the whole time?"

"I knew the whole time. There is not a dimension in this world or the next where Devin ducks attention."

"Your first clue."

"And that hospital routine. Please. The whole scheme is like Superman disguising himself by wearing glasses."

"Me and Superman," I consider the analogy.

"More like you and Clark Kent."

"That would mean Devin is Superman."

"Such a flair for misdirection," she smiles. "The ability to throw out red herrings was supposed to be a recessive trait, so as annoying as it is, I can't help but beam with pride over how you've been able to hone it with experience."

"The disguise was working," I respond to her underhanded compliment by getting us back on topic.

"It still can work. Not enough people really knew Devin to notice the difference. Besides, you don't want to disappoint the other people, or whatever they are, that you're working with on the other side."

I imagine the color draining from my face.

"You think just because I looked up that hacker..." I search for a plug to stop the leak but she calls off the search before I can finish.

"Playing dumb is even less compatible than the moral high ground when it comes to your design."

Her convoluted praise reminds me of a final play I can run.

"If you did this once," I toss the backhanded flattery back at her. "You can do it again. Why force a clone to work for you, when you can build one that's designed to work for you?"

"Too risky," she has already thought of it. "You're a sure thing."

So much for Trisha drafting a clone army to occupy Melt and his colleagues in their cubicles. Even if she fell for my fake, I would probably confess to the patch that keeps out the clones before the deception could run its course.

I hunch over and hold on to the back of the couch as though keeping my shoulders from slumping clear down to my ankles.

"Don't look so defeated," she says. "This is victory. You're the first person to ever do something like this. You're the man who sets out across the desert thousands of years ago and finds the sea, the man who sets out in a canoe and finds the island paradise."

"I'm a sucker for people who call me a person," I push a joke through my despair.

"Nobody knows who those ancient pioneers are now, but going down in history never occurred to them. There was no history. They just were. They breathed in their discovery and let the accomplishment fill them with a satisfaction few have ever known. And now you get to join that club. In this age where people wonder if there are any great discoveries left to make, and where more will be recorded in the next ten seconds than were recorded in the previous ten thousand years, you can make the greatest discovery of all, and nobody has to know about it."

"Showmanship is also part of my design," I remind her.

"That may come in handy if something goes wrong."

I release my grip on the couch and stand up straight.

"Don't throw your shoulders back at me," she addresses my posture. "All great opportunities carry some jeopardy, and this is a once in a lifetime opportunity. Or in your case, once in two lifetimes."

I roll one shoulder, then the other, as if preparing to raise my fists and throw punches. But I keep my hands down. I only want to release the tension spreading from the base of my neck. Even if I did decide to get physical, she would probably be ahead of me on that front, too. I imagine her working with a trainer every day, hitting a heavy bag and speed bag, imagining the faces of all the tech bros she wants to take out, each member of the good old boy network making an appearance for each flurry of fists and feet.

She reminds me that she will be in touch.

I nod in compliance and for the next several days think of all the snappy comebacks I wish I had thrown at her on my way out the door as I wait for the first Monday of the month.

Waiting for two o'clock on the first Monday of the month seems to take longer than the several days leading up to it.

Walking through the halls of the hotel calling out Marlowe's name in a high-volume whisper seems to take longer than the several hours leading up to it.

I start on the top floor and work my way down, hoping the portal is not in the lobby or restaurant bar. I walk down each corridor on each floor, walk down every stairwell, keeping my voice down as I hiss "Marlowe" as sparingly as possible, enough to cover the latest space. I get a bite on my third "Marlowe" of the fourth floor.

"Polo," I hear his disembodied voice from behind an ice machine in the vending nook.

"What?"

"Polo," he emphasizes. "Marlowe Polo. Like that game 'Marco Polo,' only—"

"Got it."

"But do you love it? I love it."

"Was this whole scheme just an elaborate setup for that joke?"

"Let's get started. I'm not sure how long I can keep this portal open. Ah..."

He grunts with frustration.

"Closing already?" I ask.

"No," he submits. "Here comes Rich."

"Who?"

"Richard Cloud Rabbit. The ghost who made this portal."

"Not a little girl, then."

"Close."

"Close?"

"He's Indian."

"You mean Native American?"

"Most of our residents still call them Indians."

"I'll bet they do."

"Things don't catch on in the afterlife. People do what they always did."

"What's so close about the ghosts of little girls and Native Americans?"

"It's all about that tragic backstory. People report seeing little girls more often, but according to our data, Native Americans are actually the most prevalent."

"People see what they want to see," I tell the ice machine while I lean out the door of the vending nook and look up and down the hall to see if anyone is approaching.

"To be fair," the ice machine hedges, "the images tend to be foggy. A bit of a Rorschach test. You'll see what I mean. Take it away, Rich."

A faint apparition of no discernable age or gender flutters in front of the ice maker, radiating various shades of orange and smelling of sulfur. A male voice offers what sounds like a prayer, raspy and deep, in the rhythm of a spoken-word poet.

"He comes back to protest," Marlowe narrates.

"Manners," I admonish him for interrupting.

"It's a loop, not him," Marlowe reminds me.

The voice of Rich is resonant but contained, melodic but unable to make any vibrations. I touch the glass on the face of the vending machine next to the ice maker, and feel no movement.

"So this is sacred land," I assume.

"I don't know. He didn't say."

"What is he protesting?"

"Air conditioning."

"He's against air conditioning?" I try to make sense of the revelation.

"He died installing one of the units, electrocuted back when it was new technology. The hotel was determined to be the first in the valley to have it."

"I think protesting work conditions might be more effective in English."

"He's not protesting work conditions. More like conditions in general, the big picture. He says if people need fake air to live somewhere, then they shouldn't be there."

"That's a simple, fair point," I lift my hand from the glass to touch the apparition, and my hand passes through it with a slight feeling of mist that seems lighter than it should be.

"He made up some of the words," Marlowe adds. "His language was dying, and the elders he consulted couldn't think of any words to describe some of what he wanted to say."

The apparition fades in concert with the volume of his prayer.

"Say hello to him for me," I ask as the sound and vision disappear.

"Will do," Marlowe says before silence prevails.

I stand and wonder if the portal closed at the conclusion of Cloud Rabbit's appeal, and my connection to Marlowe along with it.

The ice machine startles me with a sudden rumble and loud crack of fresh ice dropping into storage.

When its job is done and the small room settles back into a hush, I resort to whispering Marlowe's name again.

"Do you want to go first?" he replies. "Or should I?"

"Go ahead," I was too busy wondering if I would hear him to know what to say to him.

"Great news," he takes the lead.

"I'm glad going first makes you that happy."

"Your plot worked."

"My plot?"

"That's the great news."

"What plot?"

"The revenge on your friend's husband."

"Oh," I make the connection. "Fiona. Yeah. She's not really my friend. Maybe she is now. I don't know. Never even knew her on earth. The whole revenge plot was based on the man she's with in the afterlife, my friend's father. My earth friend, Kelly. She's the one who figured her father might be dead. She didn't even know about the woman you're talking about. Wait a second, how do you know about her? About this?"

"We work in a gigantic operation," he reminds me. "A universe unto itself. But we can know things about small parts of it if we want to. Flags, keywords…"

"Spies…"

"And I suppose you were never above a little spying at your company?"

"You'd have to ask Devin. What tipped you off?"

"The husband threw himself off a building that he owned."

I think back to my phone buzzing around the countertop, powered by a stream of frantic, psychotic text messages.

"Not your typical route to our desk," he concedes. "It probably would have caught our attention, anyway, even without all the monitoring devices."

"He jumped off a building?" I verify, or process, or try to make it go away.

"A building that he owned," he marvels. "Until somebody owned him."

Marlowe would not be able to follow me if I walk away.

I consider it.

"That man jumped," he assesses my silence. "You didn't push him."

"I may as well have."

"If you can have that kind of effect on someone that powerful, think of the good you could do for others."

"You don't need to convince me anymore, Marlowe. I'm trapped. Trisha knows everything, and she wants to ride me to the top of her world."

"We also know what happened to that jumper was Devin's idea, not yours."

"That I agreed to."

"And is far worse than anything Trisha will ask you to do."

"Not helpful," I glare at the ice machine.

"For a moment I thought it was," he apologizes. "Until I was halfway through the sentence."

"Has Fiona agreed to see him?"

"No."

"Now there's some actual great news."

"I also don't expect him to be here long. Nothing good makes him happy, and residents who enjoy cruelty on earth find it's not as fun on this side because the people you're making miserable aren't real."

"I should take comfort in that," I appreciate the gesture. "But I keep thinking of the texts he sent me when I pretended to be his dead wife."

"So that's how you did it."

"Devin will be proud."

"I'm not supposed to say this," he ventures. "But our new resident doesn't strike me as someone worth your pity."

"It's not him," I overcorrect. "It's the power. I broke him in about ten words. Shot him into the abyss with my phone."

"Hmm," Marlowe sounds like he may be sucking on some of the ice. "I've gone from saying something I shouldn't have to not knowing what to say."

"Maybe I can stay there next time I'm in town."

"Here? Permanently?"

"Is the idea that alarming?"

"You know about the logistical issues."

"How about after I work with you for a while?" I bargain. "Like I'm on a work visa, and I become a permanent resident."

"I know we throw around a lot of comparisons between where we work, on this side and that side. But those similarities only go so far."

"I'm not wanted in either one. They have that in common."

"That's not true."

I punch the ice machine with the side of my fist.

"Then let me in!"

The machine vibrates.

"You'll be here soon enough," he sounds as rattled as the quivering metal walls surrounding his voice. "We'll talk about it then."

"Celestial beings, higher intelligence," I scoff. "You're nothing but a middle manager."

"I'll see what I can do."

"Of course you will. You'll get back to me."

I feel like hitting the machine again, but my forearm is tingling.

"Cam Lamp is doing well," Marlowe reaches for something else to throw at me.

"So?" I refuse to catch it.

"Much better, in fact."

"Where did that come from?"

"I intended to tell you earlier, after that other news. I thought it was all good, a pile of evidence proving the great things you can accomplish on your visits."

"What's Cam doing that's so encouraging?" I soften.

"Trying out new simulations that don't revolve around his son. Moving on and enjoying his time a bit more."

"Good to hear."

"Honestly," he senses an opening in my tone. "I can look into keeping you here. I really can and will if you want me to. My concern is that since you're not a natural-born human, it may involve being an employee rather than a resident, and that means forever. No going stardust when you've had enough."

"The first time I was there, my case manager negotiated a mulligan for me, before Devin showed up."

"I know. I was on that committee."

"He liked to call it a board."

"Did that work? Make us sound more impressive?"

"In the realm of corporate language, I suppose it did."

"If I was on that committee, that board, this time around, I would have a different opinion."

"I see."

"You were still pretty new when we took that vote," he explains. "Now you've been a clone for what, another year?"

"You're getting good at gauging time."

"You've gained a million more memories of your own in addition to the ones inherited from Devin. The imprint is too large. You've experienced too much. There's no way you could start fresh."

"I understand," I complete the process of settling down.

"I'm sorry."

"I'm sorry for blowing up. I was finally coming to grips with being a clone, and now on top of that, I'm this other thing."

"I think you just came up with your job title."

"*This other thing*," I mull the phrase. "Can you make me some business cards?"

"In the blink of an eye," he plays along. "Like we do."

"You haven't done charity work before," I springboard into sincerity. "It's a different beast that can be very frustrating, and lead to a lot of disappointment."

He contemplates my critique.

Or he may have, if he heard it.

"Marlowe?" I ask.

Several seconds of silence proves the portal has closed.

I walk into the hallway to find it still empty.

Someone could have walked past the nook during our conversation and I never noticed. If someone did, they probably assumed I was talking on the phone, or talking to a person they could not see, who was just outside their frame of reference, on the other end of the small room.

Or they thought I was talking to myself, to an insane degree.

I listen to the quiet of the corridor, the sound of air circulating through vents, water through pipes, the energy of countless molecules huddled together in bunches to form wall sconces, door knobs, and fire alarms. None of this may even be here, all of it a simulation before the next round of simulations in the afterlife. Nobody there knows what comes next, any more than anyone here. One corridor leads to another, carpet over floor, floor over ceiling, ceiling over room, story on top of story, layer after layer after layer.

If there is anyone in this hotel, they will find evidence of each other now and then. Most of it will be noise. They will hear the sound of footsteps creaking across the floor above the ceiling, muffled voices through the wall, a door opening and closing in the hall. There will be occasional visions. A door might be left open and they can see inside the room as they pass. They might glimpse the back of someone turning a corner at the far end of the corridor, or happen upon another person in the elevator. They will ride in silence and look at the numbers, seeing how far up they have to go, or how far down, how many stories until they no longer have to wonder if there is anything they should say.

# Also by Sean Boling

**The Current Mr. Orr**
Devin's Best Afterlife
Once in Two Lifetimes
Revenge and Wellness in the Sweet Hereafter


**Standalone**
Cut Flowers
Abraham the Anchor Baby Terrorist
The Summer of Our Foreclosure
Satellite Campus
A Charter to That Other Place
The Latest Version of My Love Story
Show Them What They Won
The Name Field
Should
Moral Adjacent
Over Here We Have
The Current Mr. Orr

# About the Author

Sean lives with his family in Templeton, California. He teaches English at Cuesta College.